Mutuwhenua
The Moon Sleeps

Patricia Grace was born in Wellington in 1937. She is of Ngati Raukawa, Ngati Toa, and Te Ati Awa descent, and is affiliated to Ngati Porou by marriage. She was educated at Green Street convent, Newtown, Wellington, and at St Mary's College, Wellington. She has seven children. She has taught in country schools in the King Country and Northland. She is now teaching at Porirua and living in Plimmerton.

Patricia Grace's stories have been published in a number of periodicals and in five widely known anthologies : Margaret Orbell (ed.), *Contemporary Maori Writing* (1970); Phoebe Meikle (ed.), *Short Stories by New Zealanders Two* (1972), *Short Stories by New Zealanders One* (1974), and *Ten Modern New Zealand Story Writers* (1976); and Bernard Gadd (ed.), *My New Zealand,* Junior (1974). Some of her stories have been read on the radio.

In 1974 Patricia Grace was awarded the first Maori Purposes Fund Board grant for Maori writers and in 1975 a grant from the New Zealand Literary Fund for further writing. Her first collection of stories, *Waiariki*, was published in 1975. In 1976, at the special invitation of the organisers, she attended the first Writers' Conference to be held in Papua New Guinea since that country gained its independence, and in 1977, again by special invitation, the SPACLALS Conference held at the University of Queensland.

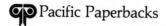 Pacific Paperbacks

Mutuwhenua
The Moon Sleeps

Patricia Grace

Longman Paul

Longman Paul Limited
182-190 Wairau Road, Auckland 10,
New Zealand

Associated companies, branches and
representatives throughout the world

©Patricia Grace   1978
First published   1978

ISBN 0 582 71762 0
Also available in cased edition,.
ISBN 0 582 71761 2

The cover incorporates a detail
from *Frozen Flames,* by Christopher
Perkins (collection of the Auckland City
Art Gallery). The publishers regret
that they have been unable to trace
the copyright owner.

To Kerehi Waiariki Grace

1

The days before my wedding were full and busy ones but more so for my mother than for any of us. It was summer, with the sun skidding day after day across a flawless ice-blue sky, taking with it all moisture from creeks and pastures, draining the hills and gullies to a sleek ivory. It was the nearest we would get to a white Christmas in these parts.

Earlier, the ti kouka far at the back of the house had given warning of this dryness, spilling out streamer after streamer of cream flowers from among its bundles of speared leaves.

The ti kouka had been brought down from the bush when my father was a small boy; in front of it stands a ngaio tree that was planted at the time I was born.

From without it has a peaceful appearance, the ngaio tree, with its tidy rounded shape and its even green. Not until you get in close to it do you discover the pained twisting of its limbs and the scarring on the patterned skin, but even so it is a quiet tree. I was named after it. A new name in our family, but I was given one of the old names as well.

Behind the ngaio and the ti kouka stands an old macrocarpa, with nodules of cones crowding the long rocking limbs and hiding among the scented sheaths of green spikes and tangles of dead twigs. I don't know how old it is. I know only that its roots are thick and heavy and that they spread wide and deep. Only that its sap flows thickly under the flaking hide and that, without its strength against the wind that licks through the gully there, the others — the ti kouka and the one that gave me the name — would not have taken root and flourished.

After my mother had grown used to the idea of my getting married she began to enjoy all the preparation and organising for my wedding. She wanted everything to be right. We bought material which I took to a dressmaker in town to make up for Lena and me. She made bookings with the photographer and florists and arrangements for the cleaning and decoration of our church and dining-hall.

My father was busy too, but I'd never seen him so quiet. It was almost as though he had hidden his real self away and left a silent stranger in his place, coming and going, eating and sleeping. It was a new mood, this quiet one, that didn't sulk or shout, cry or laugh or stamp about. One I didn't know.

'What's the matter with my Dad?' I asked one day, and he sat quiet for so long I thought he wouldn't answer me at all.

'It's all this wedding business,' he said, and was silent again.

'It's too much trouble and all that?'

'Nothing's too much trouble for my girl.'

'What then?'

'You don't know what it's like yet. To be married. Away from home.' He put his arm round me. 'It's our fault, Mum's and mine. We've kept you too close to us. You might not be ready to leave. Perhaps you and Graeme might be more different from each other than either of you can tell.'

It startled me for a moment to hear my own fear spill out into the room on my father's voice. And something made me think just then of the stone we had found, that was buried now at the bottom of a deep gully not far away. I felt a touch of stone on me, but not too coldly. Hold it a while and soon it warms, taking life and warmth from you.

'But you let us marry. You want it.'

'You'll need someone else one day. And I know he loves you very much. He's proved that to me; he has a lot of strength in him.'

I had always wanted to tell Graeme about the stone, which I call a stone to give less meaning, to simplify feeling. But I was afraid of what I might come to know about him and me, of what there could be between us, what differences. I have put many things aside over the past few years but the stone remains with me. The stone and the people do not let me forget who I am although I have wanted to many times.

'And it's your Nanny,' my father said. 'She doesn't like it. She won't come, you'll have to be prepared for that, Baby. And she blames me of course.'

Ripeka was the other name they gave me, after her.

'No doubt you are a good-looking young man,' Nanny Ripeka had said to Graeme. 'But my granddaughter should marry a Maori.'

'But I love her,' he said. 'No one can love her more than I do.'

'You know nothing,' she replied. 'Love? Love is what you're born with and what you know. You think you know this girl but what do you know? What's wrong with a Pakeha girl for you?'

Then Nanny Ripeka had turned to me and said, 'You're as bad as that cousin of yours. Never mind the Maori; he must marry a Pakeha. Both of you just want your children to have fair skin because you think that's better. You care nothing for your own people.'

And I got angry with her, and not for the first time. I was crying, and wanting to shout, to try to make her understand; crying because there was nothing I could say that would make any difference to what Nanny believed. And I thought on the way home how glad I would be to marry Graeme and get away from Nanny Ripeka and all her cranky ideas.

'What's wrong with her?' my father asked Graeme when we arrived home.

'The old lady ... said things,' Graeme said.

Then I sat down and told my mother and father what had happened. I was still crying. 'Well, your Nanny's old now,' my father said. 'and you can't make anything any different by being angry with her.'

'She doesn't have to say those things.' But my father didn't answer me. 'Well, does she? I suppose you agree with her. You think she's right.'

'I'm glad you're marrying Graeme,' my father said. 'He's a good boy and he loves you.'

'What's wrong with you? Can't you give a straight-out answer any more?' It was as though Graeme wasn't there.

'There's some truth in what the old lady says,' my father said. 'But you have to live a long time before you know it.'

My mother put her arms round me but I pushed her away.

'Let's go,' I said to Graeme. He had been sitting away from us, and for the first time I disliked his quietness and calm.

'Where to?' he asked.

'Anywhere. I want to get out of here.'

I heard him say to my father, 'We'll drive round for an hour, then I'll bring her back.' I was angered by Graeme's quiet acceptance. 'None of you will listen,' I said as I went to the door. 'Nanny Ripeka can say anything she likes, and because she's old you think she's right.'

We drove in silence for some time before Graeme said, 'Don't worry, Linda. Don't worry about what she said. We're strong enough you and I.' 'I'm not,' I said. 'I'm not strong at all.' And I was still upset. But it was fear, I think, about what she'd said, rather than anger. 'Then I'm strong enough for both of us,' he said. 'Don't be unhappy. Your old man is the only one who realises the strength I have in me.'

I thought quietly for some time, wondering about what he had said to me. And quite suddenly I felt a longing for him, which was not by then a new feeling but only new in intensity. I could feel my skin tight across my body and longed to be comforted by him and to feel his strength surge through me. He looked at me and put out an arm to draw me close to him, but we drove homewards. His body was hard beside mine.

2

I was nine years old when we found the stone. Grandpa Toki was alive then and my parents and I had gone to his place because a man from the council was to be there to discuss with my grandparents and the rest of the family a road that the council wanted to put through our settlement to open up more land in the area. My grandparents' place is a mile or so from our place, on a small rise, with the hills stacking up behind. And from somewhere in the hills comes a creek which in times of heavy rain can swell and flood the flat land of the gully.

The man from the council had his son with him, and while the adults were talking the boy and my cousins and I went down to the creek to play.

Spring was unfolding from the end of a sodden winter, pushing up new shoots of grass along the edge of the creek which was now returning to its normal flow. The wet had flogged the gully. Banks had pulled away and slid into sticky mounds along the ferny edges of the bush. Shingle, heaped by the awry spilling of the creek, had filtered mud and rotting debris into reeking piles.

I don't know who noticed the stone first. Its shape made it different from the other stones and pieces of stick lying at the bottom of the creek. Lying in the water it had no colour at all. The boy and my cousin Toki lifted it out on to the bank between them. It was about a foot in length, tongue-shaped at one end and tapered towards the other. We dried it on our clothes and sat on the bank talking about it in the way that we always used to talk about the special stones or shells we found. Or about our coloured bits of glass. Now and again we stroked our hands along it or held it to know its shape and its heaviness or to feel it warming to our touch.

Then we began to wonder how it had got there in the creek. And, suddenly, the boy, who was older than any of us, said, 'It came in the floods from the hills and it took years and years to get here. It's hundreds of years old.' He picked it up and walked towards the house and we followed with our eyes popping. Not because of what the stone was, but because of the hundreds of years and because of how it came, taking ages and ages.

'Look what I found,' he said, and there was sudden silence in the kitchen, with all eyes on him and what he held.

'Well,' his father said. He took it from the boy and weighed it in his hands, looking about at all the adults. But they too had become stone in the leaping silence of the room.

'Well,' he said. 'Must be worth a coin or two.' But they didn't move or speak.

'In the creek,' the boy said into the long moment. 'Just lying there.'

Then my grandfather said, 'It goes back. Back to the hills.' And we all waited.

'Come off it,' the man said. 'Can't you see?'

They didn't answer him.

'Well, look, think of it this way. What use is it to anyone back there in the hills. Who can see it there?'

He told the boy to go and put the stone in the car and kept talking about how they could all share. 'It was my boy who found it,' he kept saying. 'But it's your land. There's something in it for everyone.'

While he was speaking I saw my father beckon my

cousin Toki to him and whisper; then Toki slipped away.

The man was angry later when he went to the car and found the stone had gone. He accused my grandparents of many things but they were quiet and said nothing.

After the man and his son left, my cousin took the stone from under the house where he'd hidden it and gave it to our grandfather. The older ones spoke together. Then Grandpa Toki and my father went, taking the stone, far back into the hills, and returned without it. They told us how they had stood at the top of a rise and thrown the stone piece into a deep gully. And the next day they went back again with a tractor and graded the top of the hill down into the gully where the stone was, covering it with fall after fall of rock and earth.

I often think of that piece of stone lying at the bottom of the gully buried under a ton of rock and earth. And when I think of it I can feel its weight in my hands and the coldness of it, and I can see its dull green light. And it always seems that I can feel it and see it better now than I could when it was just like another shell or piece of coloured glass. As though part of myself is buried in that gully.

Whenever my cousins and I talk about that time I know they feel the same way too. And I have often wondered what the Pakeha boy's feelings would have been had he known what our older ones did with the stone. I saw him stroking his hands along the tapered handle and watched him curl his fingers about it and I wondered if it warmed in his grasp. I watched him look way into the hills with quietness shining from his face, so it is difficult to know. Perhaps the stone is part of that boy too, though I think not.

But what I'd wanted to tell Graeme during those

days before our wedding was not so much the story of the stone, because that would have been easy enough. I'd wanted to tell him about the significance to me of what had happened; wanted him to know there was part of me that could never be given and that would not change. Because of my belief in the rightness of what had been done with the stone, my clear knowledge at nine years of age of the rightness (to me), I can never move away from who I am. Not completely, even though I have wanted to, often.

There is part of me that will not change, and it is buried under a ton of earth in a deep gully. The ngaio tree will age and die. Or perhaps it will not age. Perhaps the wind will have it in spite of its protectors, or perhaps it will be in the way and will go under the axe one day. But the stone with both life and death upon it has been returned to the hands of the earth, and is safe there, in the place where it truly belongs.

3

The macrocarpa was called Papa Rakau because it was the big old one, father of the others. And it had a long arm reaching out over the track which was called Leaping Branch because you could tip it with your fingers if you were tall enough — if you could stretch up far enough, running and leaping the short cut home.

There was a time when I was too small to tip the overhanging branch, and because I couldn't reach I'd yell and cry so that my cousins would have to lift me, pleading with me to be quiet because they would be in trouble with my father if they made me cry.

Then one summer day I'd reached it on my own. One day I was tall enough to very lightly touch the drooping tip; and soon I could touch it easily. Finger-tips first and then the whole hand. Then both hands at once. And, later, two hands gripping even the highest part of the branch hand over hand, swinging, slipping down the bending green fronds.

It was summer too when Graeme and I first met. After the road went through — that was not long after the incident of the stone — other things began to happen as well. Before that time the place we lived in was a quiet and forgotten valley at the end of an old metalled road. Then after a short time we had shops nearby and a garage and football grounds and tennis courts. I was at the courts with Harry, Sonny and Lena when Toki arrived, bringing Graeme with him. I was nineteen.

It was not very often we had visitors to our club because in many ways we were still a forgotten valley.

We hadn't seen Toki for some months because he had been away working in the city. It was good to have him back again and I remember that I was wanting a chance to talk to him about all the things he'd done while he was away. I envied him. I thought it would be exciting to come and go the way he did, and thought, if I'd been the son my father had always hoped for, things might have been different. But being a girl and the only child ... and Dad being Dad ... some things I couldn't have merely for the asking, not even from my father.

'What do you want to leave here for?' my father had asked. 'You can get a good job in town, or if you like you can stay home with your mother, but there's plenty of good work in town.'

'But I want to do something different,' I'd argued vaguely. 'Be someone different.'

So I'd cried and sulked about for a few days but my father didn't give in to me the way he usually did — and perhaps I was secretly glad, remembering the other time. Instead he'd gone into town and found office work for me, which I quite liked after all, but I had the feeling I would like to do more and know more, and I wanted to *be* different.

The office was opposite the library and I went there nearly every afternoon after work to fill in time until the bus arrived. I would get some books to take home with me. And that's about all I did after I left school. I went to work, read, played tennis or netball, and helped my mother about the house. Or I went to the pictures or a social with my cousins, wondering often if this was enough for me.

There were other things I could have done but which I had stopped doing long before, at about the time when I'd first run along the track under the branch, knowing it to be there above me and yet *not* leaping to touch it. For the first time not looking up but running with eyes down, watching the track roll back under my pounding feet.

There was a concert on breaking-up day, my last day at primary school. We had been busy, my cousins and I, practising our songs and dances every evening at Auntie Heni's. And my mother and the others had been making new headbands and bodices for us and bringing out the piupiu which had been rolled and sausaged into stockings and stored at the tops of our wardrobes.

Ours was the last item in the concert, and after it there was to be a farewell afternoon tea for those of us who were leaving. That night the concert was to be put on again for adults.

I wasn't feeling well that morning, with a tight pulling in my stomach and a throb in my head. On any other day this would have kept me in bed, probably crying, and expecting my mother to fuss over me. But I soon forgot my aches in the excitement of preparation. Parcelling up the costume, running down the track to meet Lena and the others to see that they had everything before the bus arrived.

I remember two things about the concert. The first was the girl with the violin. I say 'the girl' as though she didn't have a name, or as though I didn't know her. Her name was Margaret, and she was, had been, my best friend, but that day quite suddenly I didn't know her. We had shared many things over our primary years. Between the week-day hours of nine and three we had known each other well.

Then suddenly there was a new Margaret. A girl I didn't know and hadn't seen before, wearing a ribboned frock, sleek stockings, and buckled shoes, with her gold hair falling softly on to her shoulders. And gold sounds drifting and swooping and lifting from under her bowing hand.

I felt the pain in my head climb down and crouch behind my eyes. But there was another ache that afternoon, more pervading than the cramping in my stomach or the thick dark tugging in my head.

I prepared for our item still enveloped in the soaring notes, and at the same time noticing the nakedness of my own feet stranded on bare boards. And soon it was our own music breaking in on the afternoon, on the soles of feet and the palms of hands. From the dried rolled flax and slapped flesh, voices plaiting together, under and over, the long strands of sound.

But the second thing I remember was that I had to walk away while our item was still in progress, wanting to lie down and wanting my mother to be there. Wanting to shout at her and cry. I looked into my clothing and saw the dark swampish stains and wanted to call out and blame her for what was happening. The room was swinging.

I folded the bodice and rolled the piupiu and left them with the headband on a chair in the changing room. Then I ran out over the playground and through the gate, hoping no one would come after me. I could feel all the stickiness inside my clothing and knew it would have been better to have been born the son that my father had always hoped for.

Once through town I left the road and took the short cut up the hills and down, running along the track through the toetoe and kakaho, through the creek and over the shingle. Under the Leaping Branch, with my bare feet hammering the cracking clay, not looking up. Because on that day I wished the branch far above me. I wished to be small again, flying along the track jumping and stretching but still too little to reach and touch. Crying and screaming at my cousins and feeling their hot breath on my leg as they strained to hold me.

I called to her. Calling out what had happened, with tears running down inside my collar.

'Never mind. Never mind, Baby. It's nothing bad,' she said, holding me to her closely.

'I don't want it! I don't want it!' I kept on saying, blaming her.

'You're growing up now' — trying to smile at me.

'I don't want to.'

But she didn't say anything. She took the things from a drawer for me and gave me a tablet for my headache. But I was angry with her, believing it to be her fault, so I stamped my foot as I took them from her and began to cry again.

When I had bathed and adjusted the elastic and closed the pins I went out into the kitchen. My mother had made a cup of tea and cut up some of her fruit-cake. She kept looking at me and wanting me to say I was all right and I began to feel sorry about my behaviour towards her. I bit the tablet in half that she had given me and chewed and swallowed it without taking a drink to wash it down. And I was really glad about how sour and bitter it tasted, crumbling on my tongue and down my throat.

I didn't go to the concert that night although I was feeling much better — and I don't know what happened to the small bundle of clothing I'd left on the chair in the changing room. I don't remember seeing it again.

4

I was very aware of Graeme that day at tennis; he is the sort of person you can like quickly and easily. That first time I saw him his nose was red and peeling from sunburn, and I remember noticing little tufts of blond hair on the backs of his fingers below the second joint, which seemed to matter then. He played a leaping kind of tennis that sent him bounding everywhere as though the game itself wasn't enough for the energy that was in him.

Late that afternoon we were all having a cup of tea in the hall kitchen and talking about a film that was to be on that night in town. One of the boys asked Graeme if he was going. 'Yes,' he said, 'I'm taking Linda.' And suddenly all my cousins began to behave strangely. Well, I'd say 'strangely' except that I was used to their behaviour and it was nothing new to me. First they all sang 'Happy Birthday', which seemed nothing to do with anything. Then they began to haka all about the kitchen and they followed that with three cheers.

It was a family joke then how my father 'watched over' me, and spoilt me. I had never been allowed out anywhere unless I was with my parents or cousins. I suppose for some girls that would have been very hard, but until that time I hadn't really minded. I'd joined in the funny side of it quite happily and had even enjoyed the teasing that my relations often subjected me to.

'Two lovely black eyes,' they were singing to Graeme who had no idea what was going on. 'O what a surprise.'

My face was hot and Lena was rolling her eyes at me.

In the end I did go out with Graeme that night, but not before my father had met him and had his say. I usually found that I could have my own way if it was something I wanted badly enough, and if my father could see no harm. But he was always very suspicious of people where I was concerned, especially of Pakehas.

The ti kouka is a tree with nothing hidden. It has a straight trunk, difficult to climb and with no secrets once you have levered your way up the abrasive bole. There is nowhere to hide among the upward-snaking limbs or the green tousles of heads, although long ago there had been new shoots to collect for addition to the pot, and stringy fibre with which to make nooses for the pigeon's head.

My father is a man with nothing hidden. When I introduced Graeme to him I knew he would have something to say and that whatever it was would not be said with gentleness and tact. 'You want to take my girl to the pictures,' he said.

'Yes.'

'What for?'

Graeme didn't know what to answer to such a question. 'Well ....' he said after a long moment. 'Well, I would like to ....' I couldn't look at either of them. I was suffering, knowing there was worse to come.

'All right,' my father said. 'All right. But you keep your hands off. You fool round with my girl and I'll boot your head.'

'Dad!'

'Dad nothing. He might as well know.'

So I said no more although I was angry with him. I went quickly in case there was more to come.

I didn't enjoy myself that evening and could hardly speak to Graeme. I kept wondering what he thought of us, of me; it mattered a lot to me.

My father usually went to bed before ten, but when we arrived home after the pictures that night he and my mother were in the kitchen having a cup of tea. My mother got out cups for Graeme and me and I put some cake on a plate. I could tell that my mother liked Graeme, and she asked us about the film and tried to make conversation, tried her best to show Graeme that he was welcome at our place. But my father went off to bed in a sulk because there was nothing he could growl about.

What my father didn't realise then was that, although I had reminded them often that I was nineteen (as though nineteen held the world), I was really very much younger than that in many ways. But when I tried to explain this to him the next morning he didn't seem to understand. 'I don't want anyone to hurt you,' he kept on saying. 'And anyway it's not you I don't trust, Baby, it's these blokes. Especially these Pakehas. You should hear them talk. They talk different from us — and they think our girls are a pushover.'

'Dad you shouldn't ... they're not all the same. You don't like it when they stick labels on *us*.' He looked puzzled when I said that. 'I won't let anyone hurt you,' he said. 'There's only one thing they want, and once they've got it that's the last you see of them.'

Later that morning my mother and I were bottling beetroot when the phone rang. I was skinning and slicing the beetroot and putting it into jars. My hands were all red from the juice but I quickly washed them and went to the phone.

'Are you going to tennis?'Graeme asked.

'Yes.'I decided I was going to tennis, even though I usually stayed home with my mother on Sundays.

'I could call in for you,'he said.

'Yes,'I said again.

Then I began hurrying about, putting the iron on, into the bathroom making sure all the hair was off from under my arms, cleaning my tennis-shoes and putting them on the rack in the hot-water cupboard. I was glad my father wasn't home and I kept looking guiltily at my mother, wondering what she was thinking. The vinegar had started to boil and most of the beetroot were in the pot with their skins still on, and most of the jars were empty. My mother's face was all sweaty, and she had two big half circles of wet under her arms, and two stiff hanks of hair like old paintbrushes hanging down. I found myself wishing that she would change out of her old dress and put something on her feet. I didn't like myself for thinking that way, and I didn't like myself for leaving her with all that bottling to do. She didn't say anything to me either, which made it worse. However I was glad my father wasn't there.

I was ready by the time Graeme came — and wondering whether or not I could cut up a few more beetroot without getting spots on my clothes. But when I saw him coming I quickly said goodbye to my mother and ran out to meet him. I didn't like myself for feeling ashamed of my mother — running out so Graeme wouldn't come into the kitchen.

That day at tennis Toki kept sidling up to me, banging me with his hip and making clicking noises with his tongue as though he was trying to make a horse gee-up. He had huge holes in his tennis-shoes and he was wearing a flax band on his head. I gave him a bang across the back with my racquet when no one was looking but then wished I hadn't because he went round yelling, 'Ow-oo! Ow-oo!' like a dog when the fire-siren goes. 'Ow-oo, you got to watch that little skinny cousin of mine, she's wild, man.' The frame of my racquet cracked but I knew it was worth it.

We played until it was so dark that none of us could see the ball, then Graeme and Toki walked home with me.

I thought my father would have something to say about me being back so late and about leaving my mother to do all the preserving on her own. But they were both so pleased to see Toki that nothing was said. My mother made a big fuss of him and kept calling him ugly, and black, and making remarks about his busted shoes, as though she really liked him a lot. 'Well, it's Sunday, ay Aunt? I always wear my holey shoes on a Sunday. Ay?'

My father told Graeme and Toki to sit down and have some kai. I was glad we were having stew and peas and potatoes and kumara that night. If we'd been having fish-heads or pork-bones or baked eel I would have worried in case Graeme thought our food strange.

And I noticed that my mother was wearing her slippers and good cardigan, so I knew she had known how I'd felt when I hurried out to meet Graeme that morning.

My father asked Toki if he'd been to see Nanny Ripeka since he'd come back. But Toki hadn't.

'She growls too much,' he said. 'Cut your hair. Shave that pahau off. Gee, she can growl.'

'Never mind the growl,' my father said. 'You go and see her. You only got one nanny left now you know.'

'I'll go tomorrow,' Toki said.

I kept looking at Graeme's sunburnt nose that evening as we sat talking, wondering if it was sore. I tried not to look at him too much but I felt happy that he was there with us. It was a new feeling — not a new

19

feeling to be happy, but I was feeling happy in a new way.

And that night when I was in bed I thought that perhaps I could love Graeme — later, when I was more used to this new feeling, when I could hear more clearly the small new sounds inside me that I began from that time on to listen carefully for.

After a while I thought of my father and wondered what the future was going to be like. And thought too of old Nanny Ripeka who is much more stubborn than my father and much more set in her ways. I thought of my cousin Hemi who had brought his Pakeha wife to meet Nanny, and of how Nanny hadn't spoken one word to them, but had spat into the fire and turned away.

5

I said 'the girl', as though she didn't have a name or as
though I didn't know her. I mentioned her golden hair
and the gold-threaded sounds of the violin. Yet her
hair, I know, is a soft brown.

How could I not know her after eight years? Learn-
ing to read and write together. Chanting rhymes,
singing, skipping. Losing teeth and growing new ones,
and having nearly the same birthdays. Her face was
covered in bright freckles and I knew every spot.
Knowing the green sky.

So how was it that one moment could make her a
stranger? How, suddenly, could she be standing far
above, gilded, bowing gold?

Having nearly the same birthdays and having once
been four foot and five inches together surely made us
almost twins? Together knowing the green sky and
having secrets.

Or ....

Did I become someone different as I stepped off the
bus and went in through the school gates, with Lena
skipping beside me, Toki and Harry racing each other
up the drive? Did she become someone different too, so
that we met each morning easily, hanging up our bags
and saying what was in our sandwiches?

Our eyes, looking into each other's, mingled colours
to make a speckled amber, skin colours mixed to
glowing beige as we linked arms. The touch of her was
cool.

'You're hot,' she would say.

'You're cold.'

Neither of us believing that one could be hot and the other cold. But in case it was true we'd remind each other —

Our birthdays are nearly the same.

We've got the same sandwiches.

I'm as tall as you and you're as tall as me.

We've got secrets together.

We're nearly twins.

My father cut his thumb off when he was seventeen. And it's a secret.

My cousins and I made a fort by the ngaio tree. And nobody's allowed to know.

I dreamt last night about a witch all covered in bones, her eyes were going round and round and she had my kitten in her hand.

If I tell anyone where it is they're going to ....

Don't tell anyone. About my dream.

My Nanny spits in the fire, and I had a dream too. My auntie's baby that died was floating out to sea in his coffin. It was nearly night and he had his eyes open staring.

Don't tell anyone.

It's a secret.

I won't, will you?

I won't.

Sometimes the secrets were real and not shared with anyone. Others were soon shared or forgotten. We were nine years old when we exchanged the 'secrets' that could have told us everything if we'd been able to understand. But each of us, engrossed in her own feelings, was barely listening to the other, and neither of us was old enough to realise that, though our lives crossed in one place, our jumping off and landing points stood well apart. At nine years of age we told each other who we were and why we could not be twins, or almost twins, forever. But neither of us understood what the other had said.

It was a day for running, heady and cool. Running through the gates, down the drive, meeting. Both of us running. Bags on to the hooks. Out on to the damp new grass. Everybody running. The willows at the edge of the field suddenly this morning, hanging green.

Everything's green.

Everything.

Except the sky.

It's blue.

Race you there.

To the sky?

To the willows.

Go.

Lying down here, everything's green.

Even the sky.

Willows make a green sky.

Make a sky green.

Last night, she said. My father. Showed me the violin.

On Sunday, I said. We found. Something.

It's shiny brown, she whispered. With two cut holes, like esses facing each other.

In the creek. My cousins and me, and a boy. Shaped like a big tongue, with a place for your hand.

There's a place to put your chin and it's nearly worn out — her lips were close to my ear. My grandfather's chin has been on it, and my father's too.

It's heavy, I said. If you hold it in one hand your hand will shiver. And if you hold it up high it's like looking and staring under the sea.

At one end, she said, there's a shape curled, like a new fern growing.

By the end, I said, where you put your hand there's a pattern you can hardly see. Because most of it wore

23

away long ago from people holding it, and from being in the ground and in the river. It's a curled shape, like a new fern growing.

And we stared hard at each other — but I only remember this now. We stared with our eyes widening, each of us wondering, and trying to understand what the other had said. The bell was ringing.

I was glad of the excuse, that last day of primary school, to run off without saying goodbye. Running home over the hills that afternoon I realised I was going towards the only place in the world that I knew. In the world. And towards the only people that I knew. I was glad that afternoon of the excuse to cry and stamp my feet and blame my mother for everything.

And over the next few years I decided that if I had the chance I could be someone different, and thought that it would be much better to be a girl in buckled shoes bowing a violin than the girl that I was. There was a different world that I knew nothing about.

When I started at the new school I would not be called by the old name that had been given to me. And I would not be called by the new name that had been given because of the planting of a tree. I gave myself another name, Linda, certain that this was the beginning of a new, a different life for me.

6

That night after tennis, before I went to sleep, I wondered if I would ever see Graeme again. But the next day he was waiting for me after work. He was across on the library steps and when he saw me coming he hurried over. It was good watching him hurry towards me, with the other girls coming out from work and noticing. I felt nervous but perhaps that isn't the right word. I felt excited. It was as though there was a small animal, a mouse perhaps, running round and round inside me. Running and banging against my insides and not stopping. Running everywhere.

He had his father's car and he'd been doing his mother's shopping.

'Hi!' he said.

I smiled at him but I felt so strange I couldn't say anything. It was a new feeling.

'I could drive you home.'

So I got into the car, wishing our place was miles and miles away, and hoping my father wouldn't see me when we drove past the milk factory.

Graeme began telling me about himself but I hardly spoke, even though I'd been thinking all day and half the night about all the things I wanted to say and ask about. Teaching, for example. I wondered what my life would have been like if I'd gone away from home. If I'd been a teacher. Or something different. If my father had let me.

My mother hadn't seemed to mind when I'd given myself another name, and to my surprise all my father said was, 'Every Maori goes Pakehafied once in his life.' Then he said, 'But don't forget.' He didn't explain this remark.

And after I left primary school I tried to be the person that my new name said I was, but I seemed to be confined always by the closeness of my family, by Lena sharing my lunch, by Harry and Toki always there making fun, not letting me ignore them. So despite the new name, new interests, new friends, my life didn't change much at all. Not the way I'd hoped and imagined. But I knew it would be different once I'd left school altogether and gone away from home. Away from my parents and all their old ideas. Away from old Nanny Ripeka. From my aunties, uncles, and cousins — whose very tolerance seemed to be the greatest barrier to my finding a new self.

'What's it like? Teaching.'

'Pretty good. I'll have a form one class when I go back.' And he began to tell me about the kids that had been in his class the year before. I wanted him to go on and on talking and I was sorry that we were more than half way home. I told him that perhaps I'd have been a teacher too but my father hadn't wanted me to leave home. Hadn't let me. 'Your father looks after you, doesn't he,' he said. But the way he said it was all right. There was nothing critical in the way he said it.

'I get angry with my father. Sometimes.' But Graeme didn't comment so I said no more. I was sorry that we were almost home.

Then Graeme said, 'Let's take a short cut,' and turned down Leith's road, which is an old metal road winding down to the coast. Turn left half way to the beach, go along a couple of hundred yards, and then head back for the main road again. A short cut he'd called it. It takes almost half an hour to get right round. I worked out we'd be home by six o'clock and that was about the time my father usually .... But I didn't care — I was enjoying myself so much.

We rode in silence for a mile or two, then Graeme said, 'I should take you home.' I think he'd noticed my earlier hesitation, but I didn't say anything.

He kept going for a little while, then slowed down and stopped. 'I don't want to spoil things for you,' he said. 'Or for me. And my mother's waiting for the meat and groceries.' He was quiet for a moment. 'Anyway perhaps I'm being a nuisance — hanging round?'

'No,' I said. My voice had lost itself.

'You're sure?'

'I'm sure.'

We stared at the windscreen as though we were waiting for the glass to crack.

'Let's talk for a minute or two; then I'll take you home.' And something had happened to his voice too.

His way of talking was to put his arms around me. Gently. And to kiss me gently. Then again, but not gently. Then we let go of each other, sat back in our seats, and stared at the glass again. And even though I was feeling very happy, staring at the glass and weak from the newness and strangeness of my own feelings, the thought came to me that perhaps my father was right after all. Because I hardly knew Graeme.

So when he started up the car and turned to go back I was relieved and happy, and sorry for what I'd thought.

'That was a good talk,' I said. I was happy, had never felt happier.

He didn't answer; he was smiling and looking at the road. He kept on smiling; then he said, 'I like you, Linda.' And surely now the glass would crack, shatter, fly everywhere, silver and tinkling. Now surely there would be a great explosion of glass and an explosion of colour as each spinning piece caught and held the sunlight, giving it to the eye.

But no, the two of us were riding along side by side. Quiet. Four wheels crunching the dusted metal and no other sound. Long grass on the other side leaning the way the wind had blown it. Fences leaning from want of repair. A few pine trees choked with old wood, a few faceless sheep. Everything still.

I thought then that I could tell Graeme what had been momentarily in my mind. I could say things straight out the way my father did. I could. But he spoke first.

'What did you think?'

'About what?' Could I ...?

'About me taking you down a back road and stopping the car and pinching a couple of kisses.'

'Don't think of it as theft,' I said. And it was good to hear him laugh, to watch him throw his head back, then lean forward, the car going anywhere.

'Since you ask,' I said, 'for a moment I thought my father might be right.' I could feel myself getting hot. 'That you might want only one thing from me.'

'That I'd love and leave ya' — he was smiling but talking seriously — 'if I could?'

'Yes.'

'Is that what he thinks I want to do?'

'That's what he thinks any boy wants to do, especially if he's a Pakeha. My father's something of a racist.'

This was the first time either of us had spoken any word that indicated our different races.

'Something of racist,' he repeated. 'What about you?'

'Not me,' I said, wondering if it were true as I said it. So I said, 'Sometimes I can't help thinking about some of the things Dad says. I don't want to think these things but sometimes the thoughts just come to me.'

'As they did back there by the side of the road?'

'Yes.'

'Hey, but I must say, it came into my head too. Yahoo!' he yelled, wheeling round on to the main road. We were nearly home. 'So I suppose your Dad's right. Anyway, don't worry, Linda. I mean it. Your father doesn't have to worry about me.'

So I believed him.

'Not that I'm not normal.' He was grinning at me and he looked really happy too. 'Not that I'm not healthy. ... Shall I call for you tomorrow? Say yes.'

'Yes,' I said.

He let me out at our gate, turned the car, and went home.

'He called for you after work?' my mother said when I went in. She was rubbing puha.

'Yes.' And wanting to know.

'You didn't come straight home.'

'No. We went for a ride down Leith's road.' Should I tell her?

'And what?' We talked, I was going to say.

'We talked ... and ... he kissed me ... and then we came home.'

It was no use not telling my mother.

'That's why you look so starry.' I was surprised. 'Nothing else?'

'Mum! What are you asking me that for?' I said — in spite of what I'd momentarily thought and after what Graeme and I had been talking about.

'How else will I know if I don't ask. You know your father.'

I changed into my jeans and came back to the kitchen. I spread some newspaper on the table and my mother and I sat down and began peeling the potatoes and pumpkin. Then I told her everything I'd been thinking about and all that Graeme and I had said. It was no use not telling her. She kept quiet all the time I was talking; she kept nodding her head and peeling away at the pumpkin and spuds; and before we'd finished there were enough vegetables to feed an army.

'Will you tell him?' I asked. I could hear him rattling his boots off in the porch.

'You don't tramp on a man's bunion just to hear him yell.'

'How's my girls? I thought you two would have all that kai in the pot and cooked by now. You two been yacking?'

'Too much yacking and enough spuds and pumpkin to feed the battalion.'

The vegetables had just cooked when Toki came in. He'd been at Nanny Ripeka's all day doing the garden and chopping wood.

'I had a feed at Nanny's,' he said.

'Have another one.'

'You talked me into it.' And he sat down.

'How's the old lady?'

'As fit as ever.'

'Fit, ay?'

'Especially in the mouth. Her mouth's the fittest part. Her mouth'll never die.'

'So you got a good telling off. Good job.'

'Get your hair cut. Shave that pahau off. How long you been back? You waste your money. You booze too much. You got a woman? Gee, that Nanny. She's fit in the mouth all right, the old spider.'

'I saw you,' he whispered while we were doing the dishes later.

'When?'

'Disappearing down Leith's road seated beside a handsome lustful Pakeha.'

'So what?'

'So neat, ay. I said to Graeme the other night, "You like my cousin?" and he said "Yes". "But you've got to watch the old man," I said.'

'Shut up,' I said. 'He'll hear.' But my father wouldn't have heard, not with the telly up so loud.

'Have you got a girl-friend?' I asked. I'd never seen Toki with a girl.

'I've got women coming at me from all sides.'

'Humbug. You're too ugly for that.'

'I swear to you, cuz, they won't leave me alone. It must be this sexy pahau of mine.'

'Gee, you're a humbug. You're such a liar.'

' "Get out of my life" I keep on telling them, but they take no notice.'

'What sort of women?'

'All sorts.'

'Keep lying.'

'Young ones, old ones, pretty ones, ugly ones ....'

'And?'

'And what?'

'You take them out?'

'If they want me to. The only difference between you and Nanny is she growls more.'

'And then?'

'Meaning what? The two of you have got different ways of asking the same thing.'

'Do you sleep with them, that's what?'

'If they want me to.'

When I'd found that out I thought about it for a while and then said, 'Why is it that I don't want to? You're not much older than me. And most girls my age ... a lot of them are married.' We had finished the dishes and swept the kitchen and were sitting at the

31

table all tuned up for a good talk session. 'And most girls start having boy-friends at about fourteen. I always thought they were silly.'

'You wouldn't have been allowed anyway.'

'But I didn't want to. It was bad enough having you lot around. The first one I've ever liked is Graeme and I've only known him a couple of days, so it's too soon to tell. But ... I feel as though I like him a lot.'

'Hey! What went on up Leith's road?' So I told him, and told him what I'd thought and what Graeme had said.

'But what if Graeme's way ahead of me? Like you are.'

'Like you read in the advice columns: "Dear Auntie, My boy-friend has threatened to leave me if I do not allow him to have sexual intercourse with me. We have been going together for forty-nine years. He is sixty-eight and I am eighty-five." '

I was laughing as I got up to fill the jug for a cup of tea, and wondering if Toki had forgotten the question I'd asked.

' "Can you help me? I do not wish to lose my virtue at my age. Desperate." '

'Answer me. Don't you know I'm serious.'

' "P.S. I do not wish to lose my boy-friend either." '

The jug was boiling and I made the tea. Toki began cutting some of my mother's bread and spreading the slices with butter and jam. I was wishing he would hurry up and answer my question. 'Come on, tell me.'

'Well, if I was Graeme and Graeme was me. Well .... Well .... Let me see now — I'd have a white face instead of a black one. And a smooth chin instead of a pahau one. And a skinny bum instead of a fat one. And my cousin would kiss me instead of belting me over the back with her tennis racquet. Ow-oo!'

'And I'll bang you again in a minute. Hurry up and tell me.'

'But Graeme already told you himself. He cares about you, doesn't he? You believed him, didn't you?'

'Yes.'

'But you can't help believing old uncle in there at the same time.'

'I can't help wondering. And knowing it's all new to me, this feeling.'

'Believe Graeme,' he said. 'Believe him. ... Anyway he wouldn't dare. My uncle would kill anybody.'

'I know.'

'He'd kill them first and I'd kill them second. But my mate Graeme, he's okay.'

'I know.'

'Then there aren't any problems.'

'Thank you for the tea,' my mother said, coming into the kitchen. And there were their cups of tea sitting on the bench, cold, with skin on them. I plugged the jug in again. 'You two can talk all right.' Her hair was standing out in little curls all over her head, giving her a surprised look. She emptied the cups and washed them. 'What have you two been gossiping about?' As if she didn't know! Only her hair was surprised; her black eyes flicked over our two faces, knowing. 'You missed Ironside,' she said.

I poured fresh tea and she stirred sugar into it. 'Don't think about him too much, Linny,' she said as she picked up the cups. 'He'll be gone in a few days remember.'

'Who said there's no problem?' I said when she'd gone.

'You're talking now of a different problem,' Toki said. Then suddenly his eyes popped wide. 'You mean he proposed to you? Will you marry me and all that?'

'Course not.'

'Well that's okay then. Gee, I didn't think my mate was that fast. Yowee!'

'But what if?'

'Hey, cuzzy. Now you're going too fast.'

'No. But I mean what if …. Perhaps not Graeme, but ….'

'Some other white face? Yes. That would be, yes. A problem. Yes yes.'

'Think of the old man. Think of old Nanny.'

'I'm thinking.'

'Because you know me. I'm a bit ashamed of this, but I've always wanted, always wondered, what it's like to have their kind of life.'

'I know.'

'That's bad?'

'Well, not bad so much.'

'What then?'

'You can't do it.'

'I could. Away from here, away from all of you I could. All of you, but especially them, you choke me.'

'Why didn't you then? Why didn't you go when you left school?'

'He wouldn't let me.'

'He'd have given in by now. Or you could've just gone, like I did.'

'I suppose you were right before when you said I can't. I've been kept too close to all of you. Then last year when I went away to the tournament for twelve days I realised. I hadn't been away from home before and I felt so homesick and cried most of the time. I couldn't stand it and I haven't had the confidence since. I sit here instead, shrivelling.'

'At college you were all right. All the new things you tried. Got on all right with your new mates.'

'And got on all right with you calling me black face and Harry pinching my lunch.'

'Just in case you forgot.'

'Then you getting expelled.'

'Well, I couldn't go to his classes could I, cuz? If I didn't like his jokes. I was really good to that man, ay, keeping away from him the way I did. Saving his face from my fist. "Good morning Te Rauparaha, how're the wa-hee-nees?" His jokes didn't make me laugh you see. But I was good to him, very good. When the principal asked me why I hadn't been attending those classes I told him "Sir, I don't like his jokes." So the old boy gave me the choice, back to classes or out. "I'll take the knighthood" I told him. "Order of the boot." So I was really good to that man saving him from all that violence.'

'He wasn't like that with me.'

'No, it was this big black muscly body that brought the jokes out in him.'

'And they're not all whitewashed with the same brush you know.'

'I know. Matter of fact, some of those girls you went round with. Yow! Guess why I used to come to netball practice?'

'In your mad hat and your busted shoes.'

'Guess.'

'Because my father said you had to wait for me and bring me home.'

'Yeah, but guess.'

'I can guess.'

'Yessir. Not too bad. Wow!'

7

It was nothing to say goodbye for twelve days. I kissed each one quickly, scarcely, and got into the bus. Hardly waved. Flint-eyed Nanny with her old white face, quick eyes. Enfolded in a great coat that had fitted her once or that she had once fitted into. Shrivelled ears keeping warm under the scarf knotted against a serrated wind. One old hand in a pocket keeping warm, the other held up to wave, frail as paper, a bit of crinkled litter blowing. My father was beside her with an arm to steady her and his hat pulled down. Under it his green eyes protruded like two Granny Smiths. He looked worried now, was wondering if he should have let me go, jingling keys in his pocket.

My mother and auntie, arms hooked together, glowed like twin coins. Proud, they smiled and waved, wanting to cry. And Toki turned up at the last minute. Just out of bed; singlet and jeans; jandals. Making faces and waving. Leaping at the cold snapping and stropping of the wind.

It was easy to wave one hand as the door flushed shut and the big wheels pulled us away. Sneaking to the lights and stopping, with the engine thudding softly, away again past the library with its doors still shut on the rows of silent books. And Neilson's. In an hour I would have been sitting at my typewriter watching the pages fill and would have set out the cups and made tea at exactly 10.30. A smell of old varnish and ink, and Mr Neilson's tobacco, Annette's roll-on underarm, and my own. Good to go sidling past.

Good sitting in the bus with the others all dressed the same, new tabs sewn neatly on the pockets of new blazers, and money in the pockets. Speeding up now, bowling along like a rolled ball.

At lunch-time we stepped down into nettled cold, rushing into the café over footpaths black and pocked with rain. It was easy not to think of them then, all of us together huddled in the steaming shop, and soup going down hot, puffing out hot breath. Hot breath dispersing, rising to the steam-stained fly-pitted ceiling or running in patterns down the cracking walls and bending glass.

Then finding the lavatories. Peeing together in rows, boxed. Washing, paper towels overflowing the bins in sodden heaps and our wiped hands fuzzed with paper as if they were suddenly crumbling.

And into the bus again, thankfully. Fitting easily back into the places we had left. It was easy to be warm and comfortable, launching out on to the blacked road, with the windscreen wiper making a fan-shaped hole in the rain.

Near the end of our journey the motorway was a trick wheel turning in two directions at once. Winding out cars, trucks, vans, bikes, buses. Ours was one. Crossing, changing, speeding up, slowing, so that there was no time to think of anything else. It was easy to watch and to feel the excitement, the great wheel looping down the long curve and out between the sharpening hills. And then!

Coming suddenly to an expanse of sky tiered above an expanse of rocking sea. And the hills all round, reaching up out of that sea and touching, only just, that speckled moving sky.

Buildings. Boxes, windowed. Of every size, reaching or crouching between and among the hills, still and

watching. Waiting and listening as though they'd been
caught that way in a game of statues. There was
nothing else to remember as a few lights began fer-
reting the dimming afternoon.

It was not the end of the journey, however, only the
beginning. Before boarding the ferry we sat down to a
good meal. Mrs Rowley saw to it. 'You must have a
good meal. ... You can't travel on an *empty stomach*.
... *Eat up*.' She didn't like picky eaters and in that way
she was like my father. No matter what else you had on
your mind, no matter how worried you had suddenly
become — not knowing how to order, wondering
which knife and fork — you still had to *eat*. Get
something *good* into you. Wanting to do everything
right.

At home they would have been starting their meal
too, the two of them, and Toki probably, Nanny
Ripeka perhaps, helping themselves out of the big
dishes on the table. Tonight they'd be having boiled
mutton and cabbage, and there'd be a dish of fish-
heads boiled white. The whole place would stink to
high heaven. Well. Rough sort of kai that anyway.
Much better to be sitting at a little round table for
four, eating, what was it? Beef curry, rice, and vegetables. Picking. Not wanting to finish first or last.
Watching, and wondering if your manners were all
right. Hoping the napkin you had spread on your
knees wouldn't suddenly slide to the floor.

He would lift a plate-sized fish-head on to his dish
and put salt on it. Then he'd begin expertly, pressing
the flesh away from the flat bones with fingers and a
fork. Lifting each piece carefully so that it wouldn't
break, to put it between his teeth, steaming. He would
let it cool for a moment, then into his mouth, his
expression saying that this was the moment he'd been
waiting for all day. One side of his mouth would have

small bones shooting out of it, and they would somehow land in a tidy row round the edge of his plate.
Each large bone he would take and suck; each loud
suck would cause his already popping eyes to pop even
more. And the climax would come when he was eating
the eye. A mighty suck with a great noise to it, and the
eye with all its soft flesh and juices would land on his
tongue, busting on the roof of his mouth and flowing
down his throat. Except for the little ball that would
shoot forward and pop out. Nothing would be left
when he'd finished except a tidy row of cleaned bones
and two little white marbles from the eyes.

'I hope I don't spew it,' one of them said. It was an
awful word to utter in such a place. 'Later. When we
sail.'

'It's better than dry retching,' another one said.
'You've got to have something to bring up. Just in
case.'

Hadn't even said goodbye — well, hardly. And I was
last after all, trying to hurry, rice toppling and gravy
dripping down my fork.

Then walking up the gangway, gripping my bag as
though it was the only thing left that I knew about.
Not believing the size of the ferry or the cold of the
wind cutting through or the violent stench of the sea.
Most of the others had had someone on the wharf to
see them off, someone pushing little parcels into their
hands, saying Good, Good on you, and Good luck, and
Goodbye. When are you coming back over. Over? We
were going Over. I wondered why my father had let me
come. He was at home eating the head of a fish and I
wanted *them* there waving and huddling in the cold,
looking up at me as I leant on the rail.

I saw someone then, and it was my mother surely.
But no. Pulling a little boy by the hand. I couldn't ....
Looking up and frowning into the dull light. Not my

mother but her sister, my Auntie Rangi, seeing me and waving. With her grandson Richie that I'd never seen before. My mother had rung and told her. ... She had a parcel in her hand but she was too late to give it to me.

Quite suddenly there was a wide band of sea between me on the ship and Auntie Rangi and Richie on the wharf. The tear that dropped would make no difference to the strip of water. I hoped no one had noticed.

I kept on waving towards the wharf in case Auntie and Richie had gone along to the end with the rest of the crowd, but the end of the wharf was dark and far away. I couldn't see.

Then I wondered what was in the parcel that Auntie Rangi had brought with her. Probably some of her home-made bread. She had held it up and her mouth had moved, telling me but I couldn't hear. The others had home-made biscuits in their parcels or fruit. Oranges, apples, and reeking bananas. Chocolates, a thermos of soup. Bread might have seemed — different. Perhaps it was better after all that Auntie had been too late to give me the parcel. And I wondered how different I was, wondered if I really had packed enough underwear and pyjamas, wondered if my things were the same, or different.

'Come on,' they said. 'We've got our bunks. There's yours.'

'Come on you're in here with us.' They were being good to me, but I couldn't help thinking my pyjamas might be funny, wondering why my father had let me come.

For a while we lay on our bunks looking at some magazines Georgina had brought with her. I stared at the pages, watching the print blur, but staring, not wanting to look out of the porthole and be reminded where I was.

Later we changed for bed, and I noticed that my pyjamas were no different after all and felt relieved. Having a bunk with your own locker and bed-light, your own air-vent and hand-towel was all right. Good. And having the same pyjamas.

But only till the light was out: it all disappeared in the dark. In the dark there was my father with green apple eyes, jingling keys in his pocket, and my mother and auntie laughing and waving, waving and crying. Toki arriving from somewhere. From where? Slapping his skin, hopping about and waving. Nanny with her knotted scarf, her knot of a hand. Auntie Rangi and her parcel, mouthing words ripped away by the wind and lost in the shambles of sea and waterside sound. Suddenly I wanted some of Auntie's bread. I wanted some of her bread very badly. Putting my head down under the stiff sheets, hoping no one would know.

We were Over. Legs trembling. Eyes and head sore.

Seasick by the looks .... Make sure .... Home with your billets .... Have a *good* breakfast .... Make sure. Home?

The billets in a huddle on the station platform remembered to smile. They smiled grey-faced into a grey morning, holding slips of paper with our names on them and sounding the names over to make them real. A tall woman with a military chest looked at the list and brayed out names, voice matching chest. My name was among them and I walked towards a young man and a young woman as we showed each other our teeth. Just call us May and Greg, they said. My mother would have liked them.

I thought it would be all right then, motoring through the city in May and Greg's VW, in the early traffic, with a flat sky lighting and the city beginning to yawn and stretch.

I could almost eat the *good breakfast* that May had cooked for me. Their house wasn't much different from ours. I was thinking of my mother; she would have liked to know that May's and Greg's house wasn't very different from our own. I decided I'd write a letter after breakfast telling my mother and father what a good time I was having.

I wrote to them every day, telling them about the games we'd played, describing Greg's and May's house and garden, telling them all the new things. About riding to a high place and looking down over the tessellated patterns of the city, and about the willowed river with its droving ducks and its quick trout swimming. The thin awning of smog that on a still day laid itself between you and the arena of sky.

Not mentioning how I dreaded each mealtime, choking down unwanted food, and how I pedalled to the courts each morning on May's bike exhausted from not sleeping. Wondering if he was sorry he'd let me come. Wondering if twelve days could be forever.

But it wasn't forever. On the night we went back to the ferry I put myself to bed and waited to be home, knowing I never would be. Knowing they would all have died or gone away by now. Twelve, eleven days. Knowing there was no Over any more. Only a Here, lurching and staggering above the shudder and drum. Only the vomity stink in undulating darkness.

'I was talking to Mum and Dad,' Auntie Rangi said. 'This morning on the phone. They're all right. You're not. Not all right — are you, my love? You been away too long. But never mind, not long now, no crying.

Then waiting out the bus journey in pretended or occasionally actual sleep. And getting down from the bus at last. At last. Going towards them slowly, not running. Watching my mother's eyes fill, listening to the jingle of keys.

8

'Linda's in love,' Mr Neilson said. 'She must be. Look at the tea.' And Annette giggled, or perhaps bit off one of her sneezes. She'd seen me with Graeme the day before.

Mimi kuri, my mother would have called the tea. Dog's pee.

'Found a coupla erras too,' he said through his nose hairs, 'in her last letter. She must be.' Perhaps she was, I thought. Perhaps she is.

Mr Neilson made a shelf with his bottom lip and rested the edge of his cup on it. Tipped the cup, hiding his nose, steam frosting the glass of his spectacles so that for a moment it looked as though he could be wearing a guy mask for the fun of it. 'Who is it, Linda?' Cup banging down on to the saucer and lip sucked back into place. 'Tell us ya secrets.' Unmasked but not much different.

'That'd be telling.' Which is the answer you're supposed to give.

'Mmm, that'd be telling, would it? Well, would it now?' — hunting the ledges for his pipe, thrashing his pockets — 'I see-ee, I see-ee.' Then finding his pipe and knocking it on his heel over the waste-paper basket.

The old clotted tobacco dangled and dropped, looking like a collection of dried out insect legs and wings that a spider leaves as evidence in its web. It was followed by a splash of black spit.

'Ah-h yes' — shredding new tobacco and stuffing it into the bowl. 'So that's that' — lighting up and puffing out clouds. 'I see-ee, I see-ee.'

He had put a hand on me once as I stood looking for Bordigan in the files. Lightly on my waist, for a much longer time than was necessary to excuse himself between the sets of drawers and back to his desk, testing to see which way the wind would blow. I had pushed the drawer shut and moved away, because of the hand, but more because of the gurgle in his pipe and the tangled woollen sounds of his nose breathing. Thought vaguely of my father. And thought of the books I'd read. In the books I'd read there was only one thing that ever happened to us girls. We didn't become famous or have interesting or extraordinary lives of our own, or even uninteresting and ordinary lives. We either got ourselves into what is known as 'trouble' or we lay about giving some bloke hot sex. And that was all. Nothing else. Except sometimes we did ridiculous things in Pakeha kitchens, like ringing the fire-alarm instead of the dinner-gong because we didn't know the difference.

And sometimes we were given the romantic treatment. Soft brown eyes, soft mellow voice — like soft in the eyes, soft in the voice, soft in the head. No one ever had speckled eyes like me or a voice that squeaked now and again and sometimes lost itself altogether. Or sang flat, bathed once a day, and wouldn't touch beer. Mr Neilson often made me think of the books I'd read.

'No car today,' Graeme said. 'But I could come for a ride in the bus with you. We could talk.' Without anything else to distract?

But we didn't talk. It was enough to sit in the bus side by side with our arms scarcely touching. Something made me think of Margaret then. Something made me wish that I could tell Graeme about the secret I had once shared with her.

Graeme got off the bus at our place and I asked him to come inside and say hallo to my mother. And there I was again, hoping the bench was tidy, hoping my mother looked all right and had her bottom plate in.

She had on a pair of old shorts and one of my father's shirts. Her bottom plate was in a glass on the window-sill and she was making pickle. When we went in she was pouring melted wax into the necks of jars to seal them, and the kitchen stank.

'I helped my mother with her pickle this morning,' Graeme said.

'What did you put in yours?' my mother asked. She was letting Graeme know he was welcome at our place. And Graeme started to tell her — beans, carrots, onions, cauliflower, tomatoes. 'Green,' he said as though he was surprised. 'Green tomatoes.' My mother said that she thought Graeme's pickle must be the same as hers. I don't know why this made me feel so glad.

We talked about the pickle for a while, then I walked back to the gate with Graeme.

'I go on Sunday,' he said. I didn't want to think about it. 'Tonight there's a film on. Will you come with me?'

'There's no bus tonight ....' He noticed my hesitation.

'I can have the car.' I wondered what to say. I hated my father and his stuffy ideas, and Graeme, waiting and puzzled, thinking it ended here. I knew I had to say something.

'It's him,' I said, my voice beginning to squeak. 'My father. I don't know if he'll agree ... with you ... in the car.' I wanted to say more to him, to explain, but my voice had gone. 'He's funny, got mad ideas,' I mumbled.

'Is that what it is?' Graeme said.

'Yes.' I was happier than I can say to see him look relieved. He kissed my cheek. 'Find out,' he said. 'I'll ring you. If it's thumbs down then I'll see you to-morrow.' He looked happy.

We were having tea that night and I was trying to make up my mind what I should say to my father when he said, 'I know that boy's old man.'

'Which boy?' — glad that I wouldn't have to break a silence to get to what I wanted to ask.

'That one you took off with the other day' — letting me know, reminding me. 'His father works with me.' All right so far. 'Not a bad sort of Pakeha.'

'Dad!' I wasn't able to let it go.

'Dad what?'

'What do you expect?'

'You can't trust them.' He was telling me again. 'Apart from one or two.'

I wanted to keep the peace and wait for the right moment, so I said no more. 'They have to prove themselves to me before I'll trust them,' he said.

He was in one of his touchy moods and I half expected him to begin on his old groans about land and about our kai being put into tins and them selling it to their brothers overseas, but he said no more. There was no doubt, however, that he was in one of his funny moods so I waited a while before I said anything.

'She's nineteen, Daddy,' my mother was saying. 'Don't you see?'

But I wasn't running round anywhere in the middle of the night, in anyone's car, with anyone, according to my father. Nineteen or not. No matter how much I yelled and banged the doors.

'Never mind, Linda, we'll work on it,' was all Graeme said when I told him over the phone.

I couldn't sleep that night, being unable to get past my anger with my father and hating myself for being too old to sneak out and too young to walk out, yet still the right age for yelling and slamming doors.

There was no escape for me from the closeness of my family or from the place that had my footstep on every stone and my touch on every tree. My shadow falling, no matter how lightly, across every path and stretch of creek bank and bed.

And underneath my fingerprint, my footprint, my shadow?

Other feet had cracked the clay.

Other hands had grappled the trees and hills.

Other great and monstrous shadows had raftered the sky and carpeted in great solid pile the ringing earth.

It was impossible even to escape on a dream. My mother knew every thought I had as though it were her own. It was as though the original umbilical cord had been replaced by one less visible, and I say 'less visible' because there were times when I thought I could see this new one quite plainly. And through this new one pulsed, not blood, but every thought I had ever had, every emotion I had felt, and every dream that had begun to be mine.

I could sit in my very own tree under its quiet green covers, where I alone could reach out and press a soft purple berry or thread on to a grass stalk the secret white flowers, then afterwards go inside to find her with fingers already stained, wearing about her neck a circlet clumsily knotted, matching my own.

Yet they had not learnt to follow me into the books I spent much time reading. And had not learnt to call them just 'books' but always 'your books'.

So I learnt that there was after all a place to go where I was not touched, a place where no one could find me. And whenever their closeness began to smother I would escape into 'my' books, leaving them outside, pushing them away. But wondering if this was enough for me.

The books had two stories to tell, and my family had no knowledge of either. The surface story came riding in on a riot of print which began at the beginning and ended at the end. The other story came secretly on the fingered pages, on a thumb print and tea stain, on candle grease, shred of tobacco, powdery pressed wing of a moth, and had no beginning and no end. So I could sit and wonder not only about the author's people and all their ideas and emotions and deeds but also about the lives of people who had read the books before me and those who would read them later. But that night, staring at the dark, I had no book to read, nowhere to turn from anger, nowhere to go that they could not follow.

Dreamt about the fort we had once made, under the tree that we called Papa Rakau because it was the big old one, father of the others, and it was our protector.

I was lying there alone, imprisoned by the leaning walls we had built. Pieces of dried needles were falling on me and I was waiting for someone to come. Mr Neilson came, with his chortling pipe, and hairs from his nose flicking out and back like little cracked whips, and he was holding a letter for me to type.

Then I woke with him walking towards me, smiling, holding the letter in his outstretched hand, and I remembered that one day in the fort Toki had brought his dog to show us. He had dragged the dog up on to its hind legs so that we could all be astounded by its crimson and wobbling erection.

After work the next day Graeme came into the library with me. Usually I took a quiet pleasure in reading the spines as I dawdled about among the neatly laid out shelves and the faded smell of books. But that day titles had become liquid and were running idiotically together. I chose two books at random and went to the desk to fill out the cards.

Graeme was sitting at a table looking through a book about cricket, and I thought that there must be hundreds of things that I didn't know about him. Cricket. Tennis. What else did he do, enjoy? Had he ever made his escape, and from what, in amongst the turning pages?

In a few more days he'd be gone.

On the way home we talked about the books we had read, and discovered much in common, so that my former mood was soon dissolved. I began to feel elated.

We sat in the car outside our gate surrounded by the words that tumbled about us. And perhaps it was the sound of Graeme and me laughing that put my father in a temper. I hadn't noticed his car turn in.

'There's your house,' he shouted, flinging his arm, revving up his engine, as Graeme moved his car out of the way. But despite my father's anger I could only feel elated, and I was used to my father's tempers after all. There'd be no more shouting from me.

Graeme and I followed the cloud of dust up to the house and when we got there my father was shouting at my mother, wanting to know why she hadn't gone out and told us to come in. 'There was no harm,' she said. She was untroubled by my father's raving, and now I was too, even with Graeme there. 'Next time you know what to do,' he said to Graeme. 'I won't have her sitting round in cars or driving round anywhere with any of you blokes, so remember.'

But the only words that were important to me of those my father had said were 'next time'. 'Next time you know what to do.'

Later that evening I wanted to say something to my father. I was sorry for the way he felt and I wanted to say something — quietly — to him, but I didn't know what to say. So I put my books away and sat quietly with them both until it was time to go to bed.

9

'The old man's been biting my mate's ear,' Toki said. He was in town looking for a job and had met Graeme. They'd gone to the pub to spend some of Graeme's money — to finish it all off before Graeme got away on Sunday was what Toki said. Then they'd both come to meet me.

'You know what your uncle's like.'

'We've been having a bit of a talk about the old bugger and I told our mate here that the old man takes a bit of getting to know. And I told our mate he better get back there quick and prove his shit's not yellow. Me, I'm coming back for a good feed. Got to keep my strength up. I'm a working man now you know.'

'You haven't started yet.'

'But I start on Monday. Got to get my strength up before Monday.' But I understood the real reason for his coming.

There were two flagons on the front seat as well as some shopping for Graeme's mother. Graeme and Toki moved everything on to the back seat and we squeezed into the front for the drive home.

'Never fear, Toki's here,' he said to my mother when we arrived.

She understood him. 'Your uncle he's hard in the head.'

'What's cooking, Aunt?'

Mutton, puha, and fish-heads. It was a knockout as we went in the door but I didn't mind; it was a good stink really. Compared to kanga piro, for example, and dried shark, or week-old kina, or some of the other things my mother and father and Toki like to eat.

I was pleased when Graeme said he would stay for tea. I wanted him to have some of our food and enjoy it, and if he was staying it meant he wasn't worried about meeting up with my father again.

He was a little drunk. 'Ho, getting stuck into my fish-heads and my puha, ay?' He likes to see people enjoying their food. I was pleased with the grin on his face and I tried to eat up — my father doesn't like picky eaters.

Graeme told us that he and his flat-mate had boiled mutton quite often but there wasn't any puha near their place so they had to use cabbage. My mother told him that she would give him some to take home with him on Sunday because she had plenty in the garden. 'I used to take my kit with me,' Toki said, 'when I worked for the council. There was always plenty by the side of the road as long as some other hungry Maori didn't get in before me. And when that kit was full, boy, I wouldn't let it out of my sight. I didn't pick it all just to go into someone else's pot.'

'Before you go,' my mother said, 'I'll get you some puha to take back for you and your mate.' She was sad, thinking of the cabbage.

'You know what I'm thinking,' Toki said, 'with all this talk of food? I'm thinking the tide might be right. I'm thinking I wouldn't mind a good feed of mussels and kina.' It was his stomach talking.

'Tomorrow,' my father said. It was his mouth watering. 'Tomorrow, the day of Rakaunui, the tide will be good.' So we decided we would all go to the beach the next day.

Then Toki told my father that there were two flagons out in the car. If they'd brought them in when they arrived it would have seemed as though Graeme was trying to get on Dad's good side. He would have known that Toki was too broke to buy flagons. So they had to mention it first to find out whether or not he was willing to drink Graeme's beer. You can't tell with a hard head. 'What are they doing out there? Keeping the seat warm?' So Toki and Graeme went out to get them. I felt like eating after all.

It didn't take the four of them long to finish the beer. Then later on my Auntie Heni and Uncle Tom and two cousins came in with some more and began yelling the place down because they hadn't seen Toki for a long time. 'Why aren't you married? Why aren't you rich?'

'This time next week,' he said, 'I'll be rich. I've got me a job down at the timber yard. I won't be married though. Bugger that.'

'That's a nice boy,' Auntie Heni whispered. 'A nice boy. Matter of fact that's what I came over for. Heard you had a boy-friend and thought I better come over for a jack nohi. A Pakeha too. I suppose my brother's been growling because he's a Pakeha.'

'Well, you know Dad, but he's been drinking Graeme's beer tonight, so I suppose that's something. He hasn't thrown him out yet.'

'Don't you sleep with him though,' Auntie Heni said. 'My brother would knock him down and jump on his head.'

'I'd never get the chance even if I wanted to. Not with all you lot and your big eyes hanging out.' And I tried to explain to Auntie Heni that I didn't feel up to that yet and I thought it was because I'd been kept too close to all of them that I wasn't very grown up for nineteen. Auntie Heni understood what I was trying to tell her. She's different from my father and I always enjoy talking to her.

Graeme was trying to stand up and Toki was pushing him back into his chair, 'You're not going home yet, brother. It's only early.'

'The groceries. Out in the car. And the meat.'

'Too late to think about that now. It's past midnight.'

'That's late.'

'No, that's early. Sit down, brother.'

So Graeme sat down again. We were all singing and Harry was playing the guitar. I wondered if Graeme's mother was annoyed about the shopping and wondered what his family was like.

Harry handed the guitar to my father, saying it was time we had some of the oldies. 'Where's the strings?' my father asked.

'What do you mean where's the strings?'

'It's only got four.'

'Never mind strings, just play; that's a Maori guitar. Anyone can play a guitar with strings but we experts you see ... ay, Uncle? Knock out a few oldies for us.'

As we began the old songs I saw my mother reach over and take Graeme's car keys from the table, and I heard her whisper to Auntie Heni, 'We don't want those two going into a post; they've been at it all afternoon.' The beer had cut out long before, but the songs hadn't, and as one song finished someone would begin another.

Later Uncle Tom and his family left, then Graeme and Toki went, but they got only as far as the car. Probably had a fumbling look for the keys, then went to sleep out there.

The next morning Toki came in covered in mince and I could hear yelling. He was in the kitchen, with Graeme standing behind him laughing. 'Guess who had the back seat?' And my little cat was leaping all round him getting bits of meat and going porangi. Toki had to take all his clothes off and put on some of my father's, which were too small for him. He put his own clothes out on the lawn for the cats to lick and said he'd get them later. They went to Graeme's then to explain to Graeme's mother. I was thinking how annoyed she would be because she'd been going to make a pie to take up to the golf club. I wondered what she was like and what she would make of Toki's strange appearance. They'd be back at ten, they said, and we'd all go to the beach.

My father rang his cousin, my Uncle Rawhiti, whose farm is on the coast, and found that the tide wouldn't be low until six o'clock, so we threw mattresses and blankets on to the back of Uncle Tom's truck, deciding we would stay overnight at the beach. My mother and I packed a few supplies — bread, butter, tea, milk, sugar. 'And that's all,' she said. 'If we don't get any kai moana we'll have to starve.'

'Or go back up to Uncle Ra's for a feed.'

'We can't miss out today,' my father said. 'It's Rakaunui and the tide'll be good.'

'You got to look after those,' my father said, waving his hand at the hills as we passed by Nanny Ripeka's place. 'These new roads and buildings, they're all right but that's enough now, remember that.'

It wasn't the first time Toki and I had been told this, but I wondered what was prompting my father now, on such a day. I would have thought he'd have his mind on the day and the tide. 'Those hills, there are tapu places in them' — saying the word reluctantly and becoming silent, but neither Toki nor I spoke. We knew my father had more to say but wondered why today. 'And it's up to you younger ones. You know that, don't you? You've got to hang on. Got to.' But why now? 'All that part you can see, where the bush covers, starting from your grandmother's place, then back and down this way to the creek. Then back over the next hill. That's where we buried it. That thing you found when you were children. Back up there is where we buried it, near where the caves are. That's where it came from, what you found. But it's not only that. I'm talking from way back — it's the caves, but it's all the land too.'

I felt uneasy and I think Toki did also. I didn't know why my father was being so specific: the way the old ones are when they want you to know finally.

'And the other place, it's back to the left of my cousin's. We'll see it when we get to the beach. He knows, Rawhiti does. He's had offers for it, but I know he'll never ... He could have been a wealthy man now if he'd wanted to sell. I'll show it to you. You younger ones have to know, because. ... Well, his bloody kids have all gone, ay? Stacking up money in Australia and all over the place. Bad, his kids are. They've never been back home any of them and never will be. And old Ra and Mereana scratching round over there on their own. Getting old and haven't seen half their grandchildren. Never will. As though they've got no rights. Those kids of theirs need their backsides kicked through to their frontsides.'

Off to the beach on the best of clear warm days, looking forward to filling our kits and our stomachs with the foods we liked and enjoyed gathering. Usually this was enough to set my father singing. Instead he was beginning to throw his arms about and thump the steering-wheel, and his green eyes were popping. He had been quiet lately, I thought, and different. And since the night before he'd been good to Graeme too, in a moody sort of way. He'd insisted that Toki and I should get in the front seat with him for the ride to the beach, for reasons which I was now beginning to discover.

'Well, there's a lot gone,' he said. 'But, never mind, it's all right so far. But those places. The hills I showed you and the one you'll see when we get there. You leave them. Just like they are. Ra and Mereana's kids'll never come back so it's up to you two and Heni and Tom's kids. Remember that. Leave the trees growing and those places will be all right. Leave them like they are and the creek will be all right too.' Talking the way the old ones talk when they want you finally to know, on this the day of Rakaunui, one of the best days, when the moon would be at its fullest, the tide at its lowest, and the gleaning at its best.

At the top of the last rise we drove in through Uncle Rawhiti's first gate and took the old track which was dry enough in summer to get us down to the beach.

We stopped off at the house for a while to talk to Auntie Mereana. She told us that Uncle Ra was working on one of the back paddocks and said that when he came home they would come down to the beach for some mussels and kina, 'So get plenty, you boys. Get the mussels cooking. I might have some of my bread to bring down.' She looked at Toki. 'It's good to see our boy home. If you want to leave that place where you stay you know where to come. Not much excitement over this way though for you young ones.' Noticing her sadness I understood my father's anger at that moment.

We stopped at a clearing on the flat below, which was just above the beach and where the creek came through. The same creek. From there you could see the place, which my father pointed out, telling us exactly. He seemed happier after that. It was a relief to see him beginning to enjoy himself.

It was a quiet place from where we looked out over

what was that day a quiescent sea, burning silver from the flagellation of a full sun. To the left, and seeming close, were the hills, also catching the sun's brilliance, but drawing it in, letting it filter in through every shade of green.

I was pleased to have brought Graeme to such a place, and as soon as everything was unloaded we went down to the beach to throw our lines out and fish until the water had gone down. I hoped that Graeme would get a fish and wanted him to feel the quiet of this place and know its peace at this time of Rakaunui. But the water was slacking and we didn't catch any fish. Far to the right the tips of the mussel rocks were showing and the lagoon where we dive for kina had begun to show its shape.

Uncle Tom brought his truck down to the beach and we drove to the mussel rocks. The water was warm and the mussels full-shelled. 'Carefully,' Uncle Tom kept saying, 'so you don't knock these small ones off. So they'll always be here. One bagful is enough for tonight, and in the morning we'll catch the early tide and get our kits full to take home.'

My father put the full bag on the back of the truck and we younger ones went to dive for kina. Graeme came eagerly out over the rocks with us to where we could look down into a deep bowl, starred, like a reversed sky, with clusters of sea-eggs. I told him he would need a shirt but he said it didn't matter. He was impatient to begin, standing on a rock looking down.

Then diving, and pulling the kina from the bottom of the lagoon, turning and kicking for the surface with your ears drumming, a kina spiking each hand. That was me. My cousins were more expert than I and could sit on the bottom and stack the sea-eggs against their chests, shooting upward, erupting for air. Soon Graeme could do it too.

The fire was going when we returned and Uncle Ra and Auntie Mereana were there. My father emptied the bag of mussels on to the piece of corrugated iron that we had brought to cook them on, then we sat down to enjoy the kina while we waited for the mussels to open. 'Terrible they are,' Sonny said, 'haunga things,' as we lifted the milky yellow roe carefully from the split shells and felt it crush bitter-sweet on our tongues.

'Yes,' my father said, 'that's the taste I had in mind. That's it.'

'You don't do it right though, brother,' Uncle Tom said, up to some mischief or other.

'What you mean, Tom?'

'You saw him.'

'I saw who?'

'That chef on the TV. You saw what he did to our Maori kina?'

'Yes, but ....'

'Well, you don't do it right then, do you? You got to eat flash like that chef says. ...'

'That's right, Uncle,' Toki said. 'You don't want to be a rough guts; you got to eat flash. With music, and candles ....'

'Candles be buggered. Had enough of them things when I was a kid. Set the dunny on fire once with candles. Nearly burnt my arse. ...'

'You have a lettuce leaf, don't you,' Toki was saying. 'A washed leaf of a lettuce, ay. And you arrange it .... Not just put it, you *arrange* it, in the bottom of your best crystal glass.'

'Glass! A glass is for boozing!'

'Open your sea-urchin ....'

'He aha?"

'Sea-urchin, Uncle. Your kina. Open your sea-urchin by chopping down the centre with a sharp heavy knife. Wash away the loose matter — loose matter, Uncle. All this tutae in here, wash it out. Spoon the roe carefully on to the lettuce leaf. Sprinkle with a pinch of pepper. Add a dash of white wine and that's it.'

'You see, brother, you don't want to be a slob; you got to eat flash. No wonder you knocked the candle over. I'll show you, brother.' Uncle Tom went to the truck and returned with a beer glass, then went to the fire and pulled a piece of sea lettuce from one of the mussel shells. 'Like this. See, brother. *Arrange* your washed lettuce leaf in the bottom of your flash glass, you see.' He passed a kina to my father. 'Now, e hoa, would you please open that sea-urchin with a sharp heavy knife.' My father reached for the old butcher knife and whacked the kina in half.

'Now, e hoa, would you please wash all that bloody shit out of that sea-urchin.' My father tipped the brown seedy liquid out and Uncle Tom pressed a yellow tongue on to the sea lettuce. 'Now hand the pepper here, sister.' My mother passed him the salt and he sprinkled some in. He splashed beer in on top and passed the glass to my father. 'Try this, sir, and give me your opinion, e hoa.'

'Well, chef. Not bad, especially the beer. But you starve, ay, waiting for it. My slob's way it's much quicker, brother, and you get a decent feed.'

'Ach, Uncle, you slob, what a rough guts! No wonder you set your arse on fire. ...'

The mussels had begun to open. 'Ladies and gentlemen,' Uncle Tom announced, 'the second course is served.'

Graeme enjoyed the mussels, which was just as well because he found he didn't like kina after all. His chest was scratched and sore-looking and full of spines.

One other thing happened that day. We were preparing to settle down for the night when Sonny said loudly, 'We better sleep close together tonight. Some old Maori might come marching down the hill to us.' Then he and Harry began hooting and laughing and gesticulating towards the hill that my father had pointed out to Toki and me earlier that day. 'I'm sleeping with Toki; his face is enough to frighten the kehua,' Sonny said.

My father and Uncle Tom and the others stopped what they were doing. Then Uncle Tom sent both his boys reeling with a thump on the side of the head. 'You know nothing,' he shouted at them. 'Now get to sleep before I send both of you home walking.' I wondered what Graeme thought of us.

On other occasions when we'd been to this place to camp we'd had tents and plenty of bedding. I had never slept in the open before, but I was warm and comfortable squeezed next to my mother on the back of the truck. The boys rolled themselves in blankets on the dry grass by the creek and Uncle Tom got into the cab with his dog. There wasn't a sound except for the sea quietly rattling its shingle. I wondered if Uncle Tom was scared.

We were up early next morning to catch the tide which was ebbing rapidly.

The first thing to go wrong was that Uncle Tom's truck wouldn't start, and after spending some time on it they decided to take our car to put the bags of mussels in. It was getting late. The water was right down and the sun beginning to spread. Uncle and auntie and my mother and father went in the car and the rest of us walked. They left the car at the top of the beach and by the time we arrived they were filling the bags from the cold rocks. We worked quickly because the lagoon was filling, and already we were knee-deep in the chilly water.

When the bags were almost full my father backed the car down. 'Tom,' he called, 'that lazy dog of yours is asleep in the back seat. And he's put water everywhere.' Uncle Tom called something back to my father — I don't remember what he said, but it was then that I realised how quiet he'd been all morning. I supposed he was worrying about his truck not starting.

We were all wet through by then with heavy water running through the channels. The kits were pulling at our arms and there was no dry rock to rest them on. The men held the bags open while the rest of us filled them. 'Never mind who gets swept under,' my father said, 'as long as our mussels are safe. Hang on to those kits, you boys.'

The next wave after that hit Uncle Tom. We saw it throw him forward and smash his face on the rocks. Then he fell backwards, and suddenly the water was running red. Toki pulled him on to the beach, and I suppose we all thought he was dead. He wasn't. He sat up and snorted some of the blood from his face. 'You're a tough fulla all right,' my father said. His voice seemed to have a question in it. I couldn't look at Uncle Tom's face.

Harry took his shirt off and began dabbing the blood. 'Never mind that,' Uncle Tom said. 'You go and find our mussels. You young fullas think you're smart. You make jokes of things you know nothing about and you wonder why things go wrong. Get out in that tide and find our kai, and if you drown it'll be a good job.'

Harry, Sonny, and Toki went back into the water to look for the kits. Graeme too.

They tried again and again in the full tossing tide, and I could see how upset Sonny and Harry were, but the kits had gone, pulled irretrievably down into the swirling clefts between submerged rocks.

In the meantime the older ones were talking together at the top of the beach and Auntie Heni was trying to do something about Uncle Tom's face.

After a while my mother and Auntie Heni brought the one kit that had been saved and spread the mussels along the shore where the seagulls would find them. My father was running towards the car, with Uncle Tom staggering but not far behind him.

The tide had reached the back wheels, and the back of the car had sunk quickly into the soft sand. The dog was swimming about in the back of the car barking. But no one laughed at it. My father pulled it out over the front seat while Harry ran for a rope and Toki started towards the farm.

Toki hadn't gone far, however, before we heard the tractor coming. Uncle Rawhiti had seen what had happened to our car, and no doubt had seen the boys diving about in the full tide. Auntie Mereana was with him and she jumped off the tractor at the top of the beach and ran towards us calling, 'What's wrong? What's wrong?'

'The car, that's all,' my father said. He was in a temper and he knew Uncle Ra would laugh at him for getting the car stuck.

'Never heard of a car diving for kina,' Uncle Ra yelled. 'You want to buy it some gear next time. Snorkel and flippers. Mask.' Then he caught sight of Uncle Tom's face, which made him laugh even more, and he became quite helpless, rolling about on the tractor seat as Toki ran the chain down to the car. Auntie Mereana had started to cry.

The car was soon out of the sea and up on the stony dry edge of the sand. My father turned the key and the engine started up. 'I think it's all right now, Tom.' I heard him say slowly, and I wondered if I understood. I thought I did and I was pleased to notice that Uncle Tom's battered face was getting its smile back. 'Must be an underwater car,' he said to my father. 'That car don't need a snorkel but my old dog does.' He began to laugh about old Tippy swimming round in the back seat and about his own face, which was swollen and all different colours. 'My face would give your face a go any day,' he said to Toki.

He gave his truck a good kick when he got to it and it started without any trouble. But Toki drove it home; Uncle Tom couldn't see for swellings.

Graeme and I had hardly spoken to each other all the time we were at the beach. But I had been very aware of his being there with us, and I was pleased that I'd been able to take him to such a quiet and beautiful place. A little surprised too that my father had agreed to Graeme's coming to that place, which is a place where only we go and which is accessible by land only through my uncle's farm. I wondered what Graeme had thought about my cousins and their talk, and about the reactions of the older ones to what had happened and to what was said. I wondered what he thought about us, and it mattered a lot to me.

Toki's clothes had disappeared from the back lawn when we arrived home and my mother thought that next door's dog had probably taken them away and buried them.

10

When we got home Graeme wanted me to go over to his place with him to meet his parents, and my father didn't mind, didn't seem to mind at all. This puzzled me. He'd had some strange moods lately.

Graeme's father was out front making a pebble garden. He had a barrow-load of big rocks and he was shovelling little stones on to black polythene. There was a flax plant poking up through the middle of the plastic. Their house was much the same as ours.

'You're Linda,' Graeme's mother said. 'No wonder that boy's been going round half sick with love.' My face was the colour of the beetroot she was bottling. She was wearing an old loose dress with big flowers over it. Her feet were bare and her face was all red and steamed. I began ladling the boiling vinegar into the filled jars while she screwed the caps down. Graeme went to have a shower.

After a while Graeme's grandmother came into the kitchen and when I was introduced to her she didn't say pleased to meet you or how are you. She said, 'What do you think of that pebble garden? I think it looks like a flippin' grave.' I felt dumb standing there not knowing what to say and was pleased she wasn't really expecting an answer. Then she said to Graeme's mother, 'I'm off, Mary.'

'You're taking your cardigan?'

'In my bag.'

'A warm one?'

'The blue.'

Then she began banging on the bathroom door and

calling to Graeme she had to go, she couldn't stay to see him off because she'd miss her ride to Pauline's. A car was tooting outside and Graeme's father called, 'They're here, Mum.'

'Goodbye, Gran,' Graeme said. He'd turned the taps off. 'Might be up at Easter.'

'Okay. I'm off, Graeme. Goodbye.'

'Goodbye.'

'What's the matter with you? What have you done to yourself?' Graeme's mother asked when he came into the kitchen. 'What a mess!' His chest was lumpy and red — red was the prevailing colour in their kitchen that afternoon.

'Kina spines,' he said.

'What are those?'

'You know, sea-eggs. We've been diving.'

'Yes, that's right. I saw them on telly.'

'It's a bit sore.'

He was digging at the spikes with a needle and I was wondering if I should help.

'You give him a hand, Linda,' his mother said. 'Your eyes are younger than mine. Go in the other room and sit down.'

Sitting in the unknown room digging prickles out of Graeme's burning chest. I could feel how hot his skin was and thought about him out in the lagoon diving, joking with my cousins and enjoying himself, and I felt close to him as though I'd known him for a long time and it didn't matter about the room. I wanted to say something quiet to him but was afraid he might not be sharing the same feeling. 'It's almost as bad as Uncle Tom's face, your chest,' I said.

He took the needle from my hand and put it on the window-sill, and then we were kissing as though we never meant to stop. There was a fullness in me which seemed to empty away every time I thought of Graeme going. Like the tide that rises and falls.

His mother called us to the table, which could hardly terrify me now, and Graeme told them about our mishaps at the beach. But he said nothing about my cousins and what they had said and done or about the reactions of the older ones. I was glad that he didn't mention those things.

He wound the window down and called, 'I'll write, Linda.' His breath had made an opaque circle on the pane. I could have cried at the vamp of the engine and the hiss and knock of closing doors. I could have cried as the bus blundered out on to the darkening road and away, but I didn't. I waved until it turned, then crossed the road to take another bus home.

'Come and tell us, Linny,' my mother said. She knew how I was feeling. 'Yack, yack,' my father said as he went through the kitchen where we were sitting. 'Never mind, it's good jaw exercise.' Uncle Tom followed him, proud of his face.

So I sat down and told her and Auntie Heni about Graeme's place and their garden, and told them that Graeme's mother had been bottling beetroot and how many jars she'd done. I told them about the pebble garden and what Graeme's grandmother had said, and they both changed their minds about the pebble gardens they'd been going to make.

'They do ....'

'When you come to think of it ....'

'Yes ....'

'They do ....'

'I don't think I will now ....'

'Not me either.'

68

I thought of the bus grinding away, up over the hills and down, winding the gorge, slowing down and speeding up. Stopping and starting and people getting in and out. And thought of Graeme inside the bus with his skin burning and his chest lumpy and sore. His suitcase in amongst others in the luggage compartment, and on the rack my mother's plastic shopping bag full of the puha she'd picked for him.

His breath had made a frosting on the glass as the engine trembled and the doors wheezed. 'I will, I'll write' I'd heard my own voice call as the bus bumbled away.

11

'We go down to the creek, Ripeka,' Nanny said. 'See if we got a eel in our hinaki and get us some watercress for our pot. You get a kit from the shed.'

Somewhere amongst the stored potatoes and stacked wood. The pipi and wizened paua threaded on cotton, a pot of new season's karaka berries, and a pot of the old. Two kina steeping in a bowl of water, and strips of shark hanging to dry. All the stinks mixing thickly, heavily, as though in a great acrid pudding. Hoe, rake, spade, and barrow. Hedge-cutters. Rows of jars made from old bottles for the next lot of jam, and an old bike tube to be sliced for the next lot of rubber bands. Her old straw hat. Kits all sizes. Choosing one, trying not to breathe.

Across the veranda and down the steps. 'Got a big one yesterday,' she said. 'See there' — pointing to her smoke drum where the split eel was hanging. 'Took these old hands a long time to get our hinaki up with that big eel in. Then I have to bang him with a stone so he won't get away. The creek been good to me this summer.'

She limped down the path with the knives, putting aside carefully the overhanging branches of fuchsia and heads of hydrangea, knowing, without looking down, the places where concrete had cracked and crumbled and weeds had sprung; where creeper had sent out its thick trip feelers and a branch of apple had fallen.

'Come on, my chooky,' she called, and her ginger hen came, lifting each foot and placing it down precisely, looking first with one eye and then the other. Small knocking noises sounded from behind her closed beak like distant drums. 'We go down and get our eel pot,' Nanny told it, as her cat, which had heard her call, came leaping out through the open window. 'That right, my cat. Come on, my cat.'

'My garden been good to me too, Ripeka. My potatoes, my tomatoes all good and some of my corn ready. My kumara growing, all the vines spreading out and growing good. Pumpkins going all over the place. My garden been good to me.'

'And your house looks good, Nanny, painted.' Wondering why she had sent for me.

'Our boys did it last week-end. Apricot and white. Apricot and white.' She chewed the paint-pamphlet words over on her old gums. 'Yes, apricot and white.'

I pulled the hinaki up on to the bank for her and went to cut watercress while she scraped and split the small eel that was in it, wondering, yet knowing, why she had sent for me. 'Nanny's been asking for you,' my mother had said. 'You haven't been over for a long time.'

'She growls too much,' I'd said.

'Never mind that. We won't have her for ever.'

'And old ideas worse than Dad's.'

'You got to listen to the old ideas while you still got a chance.'

So after work that day I packed a few things in a bag and walked the mile to Nanny's. When I arrived she was bending and poking sticks into her range. 'About time,' she grumbled as she put her arms out to me. 'About time you come' ... and I waited for her to say more, but all she said was, 'We go down to the creek, Ripeka. See if we got a eel in our hinaki.' I wondered yet I knew.

The eel was clean now, scraped and opened, the

translucent flesh revealed. She was feeding little pieces to her hen and cat which were snatching and pecking at her hand. 'The creek been good to me again,' she was telling them. 'Now I go and put this one in the salt and take our other one inside. Not for you to eat all, my chooky and my cat.'

I helped her to her feet and we returned slowly to the house.

After tea she began to tell me the old photographs, which I already knew, fading on every wall. Tell me who they were and what they were to me. Then she told me of the ones before that, who were not on the walls but whom she had known. Then back before that to the ones she had never known or seen. And her voice that had been slow at the beginning and thoughtful began to chant out the ancient names coming from far back, so I could know them. I was beginning to know them because I had heard them many times before. Beginning to know, yet knowing there was more to understand.

Thus the room had become filled with people. We sat quietly among them as they sat shawled and silent in the now silent kitchen.

Then after a long time Nanny said quietly, 'Mummy said you got a Pakeha boy-friend.' It *was* why she had sent for me. I wouldn't look at her. 'Why the Pakeha?' But I couldn't answer. 'What's wrong with the Maori?'

'Nothing. Nothing, Nanny. But Graeme, he's all right. He's not like you think.' But she let out her breath disapprovingly and was quiet for a long time. 'Bad as your cousin,' she said finally. 'You think a Pakeha is better and you think you can be happy, but you know nothing.'

'Those are old ideas,' I said, feeling my anger.

'Old ideas you think. You do what I tell you and get a Maori boy-friend.'

'What for?' Not stamping my foot and not yelling at her. 'I happen to like Graeme.'

'Happen to like, happen to like, what's that talk? You talk like them already. All right for a little while, then he leave you. Give you a baby, then go.'

'You're wrong' — and I wouldn't shout — 'You're wrong,' I said quietly. 'You and Daddy think the same old things, but you, Nanny, you're worse than him, and you're both wrong.' I was beginning to cry from needing to stamp and shout, but there would be no more of that from me.

And I thought of Graeme and wished that we could be together somewhere, riding about in his car and talking, or watching the sea and smelling its salt smell, or holding each other closely as we had on that last afternoon. Instead of being in that faded spooky kitchen with burnt wood dropping through a broken grate, and bags spread over the worn patches in the lino, my forbears staring down through the gloom at me, disapproving, and the old names and the names before that still sounding from the walls and corners.

'He's gone now, this Pakeha?'

'He's coming back.'

'We'll see, we'll see.' And was quiet for a long time, sitting on her stool by the range and letting the old hands rest like two pale spiders on her lap. 'There's nothing wrong with a Maori boy,' she said. And when I looked at her she was so very old and small that I felt all my anger dissolving.

So I asked her — because I really wanted to know — I asked her not angrily, 'Why is it that you dislike the Pakeha so much?' And she thought about what I'd asked. Thought for some time. 'I don't hate,' she said at last, because the other word was new to her. 'I don't hate. I like the Pakeha and all these things he made. My warm house, my warm bed, my old stove, a fridge for my kai, a radio for my ears, and new eyes to help my old eyes see better, and Pakeha things to help my garden grow, and all sorts of flowers for me to look at, and to take to my family buried over there. I don't hate.'

'Then why?'

'Because. You younger ones, like your cousin, you're giving our blood away. You want to make us weak. Those old things I tell you, you want to make them into nothing. There's nothing wrong with a Maori boy,' she said, 'nothing wrong with a Maori,' looking so full of sadness I could have cried.

I washed the few dishes, tidied the bench, and went out to the porch. Then carefully, so as not to disturb her old chook that perched there, I picked up the bundle of sticks for the morning fire, brought them in and put them down on the hearth, careful not to disturb her cat that slept there.

I wanted her to say something to me and to know that things were all right between us, 'You should get you an electric stove,' I said, to move away from what I could not or would not understand. 'Tell Daddy to buy you an electric stove.'

'The electric, it cooks the kai,' she said, 'but the bones stay cold.'

Perhaps she was right; it was warm and comfortable there in the kitchen. 'And here, I nearly forgot,' I said, bringing my bag from the bedroom.

'You got something for me?'

'Chocolates. And some magazines.'

'Good, Ripeka, you find my glasses. On the sideboard so I can read my books. So I can look at all these pretty clothes and these lovely houses and furnitures. But you remember what I say, Ripeka.'

'And teeth, Nanny, you need teeth. Some of these chocolates are hard in the middle.'

'My teeth is no use to me, Ripeka, for eating. My teeth is just for smiling at people when I go out somewhere. My chooky and my cat don't know me with teeth.'

'Come on then, I'll help you.'

I brought her nightie out and warmed it, then she changed by the fire and I helped her into bed. I was sad because she felt so small and thin through her old nightie, not much different from the little bundle of morning sticks I'd brought in and put down on the hearth.

I tucked the sheet in and put a magazine in her hand. She closed her old gums on the chocolate I had chosen for her and let the caramel flow.

I went out on to the veranda for a while, looking out over where I knew the river to be and out towards the blackness which was the hills.

There was no light at all, it being the night of Mutuwhenua, when the moon is hidden, when the moon goes underground to sleep. And in the darkness my thoughts were a confusion, thinking of what the old lady had said to me, thinking of my father and of what the past had given me and of what the future held. Then I thought of Graeme again and wished that he could be with me and that we could talk together about all the things we hadn't had time for.

His letter had arrived the week before, my name and address large and bright on the whiteness of the envelope. Surprising me, because I felt I'd known Graeme a long time and now I was seeing his hand-writing for the first time. And his writing was so large and sure I was afraid for a moment to take the letter down from the window-sill.

Telling about the journey home and how pleased his friend had been with the puha and what a good meal they'd had. About his new class and the new room he was in, and little things about the children that made me want to laugh and cry. How sore his chest had been until Manuel had helped him to get the remainder of the spines out, and how his friend had laughed at him, especially when he found out Graeme didn't like kina after all.

Reading the lines of large handwriting was like hearing Graeme's voice again. And the beach '... more quiet and beautiful than any place I've ever been. ...'

'You know that night on the beach? I didn't understand at first why your Dad and Uncle Tom were so angry with Sonny and Harry for the things they were saying. And I still don't understand but I think I could one day. I didn't realise until next morning how serious they were. Even when your uncle let fly I didn't realise. And I don't know if it is in me to believe such things; yet who am I not to believe when there are so many things not understood. I felt an uneasiness that was nothing to do with angered spirits. It was a feeling that perhaps I shouldn't be there with you at all. That it wasn't my place. I felt properly on the outside for the first time. Even your father's suspicion of me hasn't really touched me, not deeply, not yet. But that day? I wondered how you felt. You were very quiet, Linda.

'How is Toki? Do you know what I've been thinking? I think he came home from the club with us that night so he could protect you in case I was some raving body-snatcher, or so your father wouldn't be angry. And I think he came back with us that Friday to smooth things over. Well, I might be wrong, but I think if I rode through there on my horse, snatched you up and rode off into the sunset, I'd have a posse on me in no time.

76

'Write to me, Linda. I miss you. Tell me all the things in the world that we never had time to talk about. I wonder if Toki found his clothes? Please write, Linda. ...'

I wrote to Graeme about the ordinary things. About my work and the people there, about the books I'd been reading, and about the new tennis racquet I'd bought. And while I was writing I kept wondering how I could answer what most needed to be answered. It was as though I could hear his voice: 'You were very quiet, Linda, and I wondered how you felt.' How?

'... I think more than anything I worried about what you would think of us' I wrote, 'which I suspect was wrong of me. You said you didn't know if it was in you to believe such things — well, I know it *is* in me, and yet on that day I was not afraid, I felt a sort of safeness. And there is a story that perhaps one day I will be able to tell you.'

If I was away from them, and this place, I thought, my life would be different. Away from here I don't know how I'd feel, looking back.

Looking out from the veranda into the darkness to where I knew his grave to be, I thought of Grandpa Toki. I had not been afraid either on the night of Grandpa Toki's death. I had not been worried by the tapping on the pane and the sudden warm feeling that had come over me. We were in our kitchen at home preparing food for relatives who had come to see old Toki who was very ill. We were sitting down to eat when there were three sharp taps on the window by the table.

So we listened for the footsteps on the path, waited for the door to open, wondering who it was. But no one came. Then we heard the tapping again. And my father pulled the curtains aside and looked out on to the patch of light that shone on the ground but could see no one. There was a warmth in the room.

My father and uncle went out and round the house, then stood for a while, listening and talking. Then my father came back to the doorway and said, 'I think it's the old fulla.' And as he was saying it the phone rang.

It was not something to make you afraid. I was glad the old man had stopped to say goodbye.

The only strangeness came later, going into his and Nanny Ripeka's house and not seeing him there. Seeing his old place on the veranda empty and thinking of his old body crumbling under the ground as though it hadn't been anything at all.

But sometimes I know he is still there after all, and when I hear the older ones talking about him I feel I know him in a way I never knew him when he was alive. As though all the talking is his spirit and is what is keeping him close to all of us. And sometimes when I think of him I see him on a hill with something in his hands. Something that he takes and places down in the gully before they send the rock and rubble over, and I feel the same warm feeling.

But I could write nothing of this in my letter to Graeme even though I did have the feeling of wanting to tell him something special. Something about me and about us, but I was afraid to find out how far apart we might be, remembering Margaret.

Instead I told him of my visit to Nanny Ripeka's and described her place to him and tried to explain what she was like. I told him some, but not all, of what she had said to me.

The other thing I told Graeme about was Toki's clothes. 'We heard shouting, and when we went out to see what was wrong we saw a neighbour from down the road running towards our place, very upset, shouting and waving something. Her face was all red and she was out of breath. So we sat her down on our rubbish bin to recover. She had one hand on her chest and in the other she was flapping these rags. "Blood-stained clothing" she was gasping. "Under my hedge ... Blood all over .... Blood-stained clothing half buried .... At my place, under my hedge ...."

' "Those are Toki's" my mother told her. And our neighbour began to scream again because she likes Toki. It took ages to calm her down and explain. ...'

Nanny was up before me next morning. The kitchen was warm and there was a smell of eel baking. The kettle was already on the boil. Out in the porch her impatient chook was scratching at the doorstep and tapping its beak on the door. 'Make you some kai,' she was saying. 'To take to your work. Get you some cold eel and some corn and a bread from the cupboard. Wait on, my chooky.'

I kept thinking of my cousin and his wife who had never been back to see Nanny since she had shown her anger and disapproval. I wondered what his life was like now and wondered if he could be happy away from all he'd ever known.

There was another question I needed to ask Nanny Ripeka but there wasn't time.

'You remember, Ripeka, what I tell you,' she said as I went out the door.

12

A cold wind was snapping at the streets and every gust had on it a hint of rain. In the meantime, since the rain had not yet arrived, the wind whipped up the street's debris, shuffling it along the footpaths and gutters, tossing it out on to the roads, flattening it against walls and fences, then snatching it away again. The old tickets, pie bags, lolly papers dodged here and there at the head of the wind like mice in a maze and came to rest finally huddled against the wall of the waiting-room, in the long grass that had grown up through the gravel and old tar. Along with the smashed bottle and oil patches, and the little spurts of pee from dozens of dogs. The loaded cars were heading for the main road, their occupants watching the sky and hoping. The buses bumbled in and out, bringing some, taking some, and all of them looking at the sky to confirm what the wind had already told.

The letter in my pocket told me what time Graeme's bus would arrive, and the day before I had looked forward to this moment. All week I had been impatient for this time to come. But now, sitting in the waiting-room where the wind explored every corner, where people came and departed with their bundled belongings, and buses trundled in and out, I began to wonder what we would have to say to each other.

I had expected to see some of his family waiting for him but now I was glad there was no one to know my foolishness. Because I had forgotten what he looked like. Trying to picture him in my mind all I could see was a size and a shape. The letters which had meant so much to me over the past weeks suddenly seemed the only real things. If we came face to face right then we would be strangers to each other. Foolish to be sitting in the half-light of a cold and cloudy afternoon waiting for someone you didn't know and who wouldn't know you — whose face you could not recall and whose voice sounded only from a bundle of pages. Waiting for the rain to come.

But it was too late to walk away. The bus had opened its doors and he was getting out, waiting for his luggage. His face, which I remembered after all, was thoughtful, even sad, as he waited, not looking about him, for his luggage. Not looking for me and not expecting anyone, but it was too late to walk away.

I sat quite emptily, wondering what would happen, wondering what could be between us.

'Hallo, Linda,' he said.

'Hallo.' But I don't know whether I spoke the word aloud or not, and we sat like two sad people who have nothing to say to each other, who have forgotten what there was between them. Greeting each other politely, and sitting, not closely, staring out at the dejection of sky leaning heavily into the grappling wind.

Then we were walking, nowhere it seemed. Or perhaps everywhere. Searching and wondering if we could find and recognise each other again. A large drop of rain splashed on to the path in front of us.

Sitting facing each other across a table, thinking of polite things to say.

'Do you want ... a pikelet? Anything?'

'Just coffee.'

'Just coffee, thanks.'

'Two. Two coffees. Please.'

There had been so much, yesterday, to say. But now, was now. ... And the rain had begun. Tears on glass. Which was a relief. It was a relief, the rain.

'It's raining.' And then it was all right, this silence between us, and he seemed to know it too, putting an elbow on the table and resting his chin on his hand. Our coffee was from the same jug, only the cups were different, and the first mouthful went down scalding hot.

'Yes, rain.'

'I was afraid you wouldn't come.'

'I was afraid I wouldn't know you.'

'The coffee ....'

'It's hot.'

'But you were there.'

'And I did. And you see I really wanted a pikelet. Please.'

'Yes, pikelets. And savouries. And sandwiches.' All piled on one small plate, and the pile beginning to topple. 'Made it. You never thought, did you?'

Then talking, as though words were rain. Distantly we could hear its thrum.

And long afterwards someone began dimming the lights and stacking chairs, bringing out the mop and bucket. We stood up to go. 'I don't know how it will be, but I do love you. A lot, Linda.'

I ran out and along the drenched footpath, afraid, and wondering how it would be, Graeme struggling with his suitcase against the weather and hurrying after me.

'You didn't answer,' he said, as the taxi pulled away.

'It's running in rivers everywhere. Off you, off me, off your hair and off mine. The seat, it's soaking wet.'

'You didn't, you just ran.'

'In the rain.'

'Without answering.'

'Because you didn't ask. Anything.' And because I was suddenly afraid. Not knowing how it would be. Not knowing what the rest of my life would be like.

'And now we're both wet, water running, and your hair. If I dry your hair for you will you tell me that you love me? It's the only thing I want to know.' Rubbing my hair with his sleeve, almost angrily. 'I do, I do love you,' I said. Loudly, scaring myself with the loudness of my own voice — and wondering.

13

'There was that beauty queen,' my mother said, but he didn't answer; he was in one of his moods. He'd been like that all through breakfast, still angry with me coming in so late and wet through. 'You know, the beauty queen.'

'What beauty queen? What are you talking about?' he mumbled into his mug of tea.

'Remember, that Pakeha girl who used to be always riding round on the back of your bike. That beauty queen.'

'Mum, what are you talking about? Dad couldn't have a beauty queen riding round on the back of his bike.'

My father couldn't help himself then, 'We were just good friends,' he said.

'Just good friends!' my mother and I said together to help dissolve his mood. 'Where do you get your words from, Dad? You've been reading love comics again.'

'She was in the beauty contest that used to be on in town in the summer,' my mother said. 'Very pretty, with beautiful flash clothes and a lovely figure and small feet.'

'Mum, stop lying. What would a beauty queen be doing ....'

'I won her in a fight.'

'You don't win beauty queens, Dad, in fights.'

'Outside the old hall in town there. Got bored with the dance, sick of smiling at people, so I went out and stood in the doorway. Thought I might get on my bike and go home or look for a party somewhere. This fulla I went to school with came out with a girl and he saw me standing in the doorway. Well, I'd never liked him you see and I suppose I was in a bit of a liver from smiling at people too much. Thought to myself I'll move when he asks. I'll listen to him use his manners in front of that pretty girl. "Out of the way, hori" he said. So that was excuse enough, ay? I went outside ahead of him like I was a very obliging hori, then I turned round and smashed his face. God, it was soft! That's the softest face I ever .... One hit and it busted. I never seen a face like it, even your Uncle Tom's .... was nothing. And that girl was standing there shaking and crying. Well, I felt sorry for her, felt bad having all that enjoyment at her expense. "I'll take you home" I said. "On my bike." I didn't think she would but she did. We took off on my bike while her boy-friend was still picking himself up off the ground and she was after me all the time after that. Course I wasn't bad-looking those days, before my chest slipped to where it is now, before your grandfather broke my nose. Could hardly get my clothes on for muscle those days.'

'And you and her did some pretty bad things together?'

'Course not.'

'Course you did. You didn't make all those things up that you think about people. You must have.'

'Course not. Well, only some.'

'The rest was in his mind.'

'So you and her started going round together.'

'For a while. Her and I, we got on all right together, till she took me home to her place, and till we went to that funny party. ... That's what opened my eyes. That's why I think the way I do. Sometimes.'

'Did you tell Nanny and Grandpa?'

'Do I look stupid?'

85

'Not all the time.'

'They found out but not till later, lucky for me. That's why they were glad when Mum and I ....'

'Did she win the contest?'

'Yes, she won and her old man put on this party for her. That Saturday morning I was playing rugby and after the game she asked me to come over to her place for lunch. Well, I was pretty scared but I cleaned myself up and thought I didn't look too bad. Course that was before my chest, and my nose. And we went to her place on my bike. I was scared but I thought the girl was pretty brave taking me home.

'When I got there her mother spoke to me. Smiled. And I smiled. Then her father shook hands. Smiled. Same with her brother. I thought it a bit funny her father smiling, shaking hands, saying polite things, when he should have been kicking my teeth for some of the things I'd been thinking about his daughter. ...'

'You see, Dad. I told you, ay, Mum?'

'Tomato sandwiches we had. And I was so scared of their cups and saucers and her old man smiling so much that my bread kept sticking down my throat and I couldn't talk.'

'Then you had a party?'

'That night. Tried to get out of it. I was still scared. Thought her old man was probably saving one up for me. The smile was just the softener. How could he be pleased at me taking his beauty queen daughter all over the place and me thinking the things I was thinking. Her too.

'Well, I got there and I got a bit of a shock. Her old man wasn't there, neither was her old lady. No grown-ups at all. Only a whole lot of young ones standing round in little groups boozing, and a record playing on their gram. Two or three couples were dancing on the flash carpet with their shoes on; well, it was all strange to me those days. I asked her where her Mum and Dad were and she said they knew when to make themselves scarce. I didn't want to sound dumb so I said no more and started doing what everyone else was doing, which was mainly talking and boozing in these little groups.

'Then after a time these little groups started breaking up and couples were getting into corners kissing and hanging on to each other. Others were horsing round spilling booze and switching the lights on and off. But I kept expecting her father to come in and kick us all out; I thought he'd come in yelling any minute; but the girl was quite happy boozing up like everyone else.

'Then later I went outside for a mimi and there were these couples rolling under the hedge. Only the feet showing. This Maori had his eyes opened that night. Then I went inside, and before I got to the room where the rest of the crowd was I heard the girl call me from one of the bedrooms. I went in and she was sprawled on a bed. Waiting for me, she said. You didn't see this Maori for dust, no matter what thoughts I'd had before that. Out the door, on the bike, and away. That was the last .... After that your mother, she started chasing ....'

'Don't lie.'

'All right, darling.'

'Darling nothing, you liar.'

'Don't hit me, darling. You know you used to bring me cake when we were at school.'

'You used to pinch it off me, you liar.'

'And grapes. You used to bring me grapes, ay dear?'

'Dear nothing. You used to pinch them off me. That's why I punched your mouth one playtime.'

'That's love.'

'And you been scared ever since.'

'Don't hit me, darling. Just kiss me sweetly like you did that time under the apple tree.'

'You liar.'

'Did you kiss him under the apple tree, Mum?'

'Don't listen; he's lying.'

'After the pictures on Saturdays I used to take her home on the bike. They lived the other direction from town, down the main road. You've seen the old place. I'd take her home on my bike, then we'd wait down at the bus stop so her father wouldn't know she hadn't come home in the bus. Then when the bus arrived we'd walk along with the others. There was an apple tree not far from her place, and I'd leave her there and go back down the road to where my bike was.

'Well, one night we got so interested in our kissing that your mother forgot to let go of me. Don't hit me, dear, you know I'm telling the truth. Then suddenly her old man was there, don't know how, but there he was. He broke my nose first, then he kicked his boot so far up that it hit my backbone. I had to lay down for an hour before I could move enough to get myself home.'

'But you went back again?'

'The next day. Your Auntie Heni and the others they all laughed at me the next morning because they guessed what had happened. And I was wild. For a while. Then I had to admit to myself I deserved all I got. And I made up my mind I'd marry your mother.

'You know what I did then? I put on this white shirt that I'd bought for Heni and Tom's wedding, and I didn't want to wear the bow-tie so I sneaked into the old man's wardrobe and got out his black tie that he wore to funerals. I polished my shoes up and combed my hair. Then I put a cap on so my hair would stay neat and tucked my trouser legs in my socks and went off to her place on my bike.

'I roared up their road, revving as loud as I could, then I got off, took the trouser legs out of the socks, straightened the old tie, and took the cap off and patted the hairdo.

'Your grandfather and your mother's two brothers were in the back garden hoeing. And I knew her brothers were laughing at me but I walked, or limped, over to where the old man was. ... He was a lovely talker the old man. I wish you'd known your other grandfather, Baby. He had a quiet voice, you know, and a way of saying. Leant on his hoe and looked at me. "Back for more" he said. "And already dressed up for your own tangi I see." Your uncles were splitting their sides. "I want to marry your daughter" I said. I didn't like to say your mother's name so I said "your daughter". Well, the old man just looked at the ground and kept on hoeing, and your uncles looked as though they needed a pee. "Get him a hoe" he said to one of them. And when we'd weeded half the garden he said, "What for? What have you been up to with my girl?"

' "Only what you saw" I said. So we kept on with the weeding. He was hoeing fast and it wasn't easy keeping up with him because of my sore back and my nose almost covering one eye. "Give me a good reason" he said. Your uncles were hoeing fast too so they could keep listening, to see what else there was to laugh at.

'At first I was going to say, "because I love her", like they do in the pictures, but I thought he would laugh at that. I kept weeding along the rows thinking of a good reason. Trying to sort out my reasons. And all I could think of was her and me the night before under the apple tree kissing and forgetting to stop, and her forgetting to let go of me. Then I said, "Because I want to get along a bit better than what you saw" — thinking what other reason could there be; if he's going to hit me he'll hit me now. Your uncles stopped work and waited for the excitement. The old man stopped hoeing and looked at me for a while. Then he said, "It's more than a bike you've got between your legs then." '

My father stopped talking and was quiet. After a while he said again, 'I wish you'd known him, Baby. I've never felt prouder than when he said that. He was letting me know he thought I had guts — balls you might as well say. Your uncles thought he was telling me I was randy and they were waiting for the connection — his fist, my face. But I understood. We always understood each other your grandfather and I.

'When we finished the hoeing we went inside. Your Mum and your grandmother were cooking a feed. And when we were all sitting down at the table he nodded his head towards me and said, "This one wants to marry our girl." Your mother wouldn't look at me and no one spoke for a long time. Then your grandmother said, "There's nothing against it, and she's old enough."

'Your grandfather asked Mum if she wanted to marry me. You know what she said? She said, "I suppose so." '

'Well, I thought it would stop him pinching things off me and being a nuisance, and I could give him a hiding whenever I wanted to.'

' "You bring your old man and old lady over one day soon and we'll talk" he said. That's how it was done those days.'

There was a question that I wanted to ask my father but he went on. 'When I told your Grandpa and Nanny they talked about it together and said they would visit your mother's place. They said there was nothing against it. And your Mum and I were married not long after that.'

'And we'll get divorced in a minute if you don't get away from the table. They'll be here in carloads soon. This isn't an ordinary week-end you know.'

'And only one little girl to show for it. Had to wait ten years ... for our girl.'

'Easter. All your relations will be here any minute. ...'

'Your Mum, she's been growling ever since. I don't know why I married your Mum. ...'

'Any minute. Yelling the place down. ...'

'I knew I should've married that beauty queen.'

'You should've too.'

'Plenty of money that girl.'

I was pleased to hear them bickering at each other even though there was a question I had wanted to ask my father.

'This boy Graeme, he'll be coming to see you. Well, I don't mind and things are different these days. As long as he's good to you, that's all.'

Easter passed the way it usually did at our house, with people calling in, passing through, or staying. That Friday it rained and a bladed wind cut through the gully in long swipes, yet it was warm enough. I was warm.

Auntie Pare and Uncle Hemi were the first to arrive, shaking off drops of rain, stamping away the cold, and complaining that the weather wasn't too good, brother, sis, for the time of year.

But warm inside with the walls and ceilings beginning to sound and the pots on to simmer, huffing steam as Auntie Pare lifted the lids to pry. Opened the oven to pry. 'Fruit-cake, Linda. I say, your Mum's fruit-cake. I know the right time to come.' And in the deep-freeze. 'I say, I knew you'd have eel and water-cress frozen, and fish-heads and paua and corn. We brought some crayfish with us, six big ones, fresh cooked yesterday in our big pot. Put a couple in here in your deep-freeze, and put the rest on the table for when those others come. I say, you know what Lena told me in her letter?'

'Yes, I know, Auntie. He'll be here later.' For you to look at, I thought, pry at — I sa-ay.

'It's true what our niece wrote to me then? That's what I came for. And to see all of you of course, and help with the digging of course. But it's true, ay? I say, what does your Dad ....'

'He hasn't given him a black eye yet. Hasn't turned him out.'

'I sa-ay. But your Daddy's not looking so well; he better keep his hands down now, Linda. He's a bit skinny you think. And quiet.'

'He hasn't done so much yelling lately. Nor have I.'

'You? You're a young woman now. And a boy-friend, I sa-ay. I didn't think he'd ever let you have any boy-friend let alone a .... Oh I sa-ay, I bet you old Ripeka don't know.'

'She knows but I think I'll keep out of her way for a while.'

'That's right; you keep out of her way. They don't understand, these old ones. It was hard enough in our day to know who. And to know there was nothing against ..... Unless you knew all the old things, then there was no way for you ... until the old people got their tongues going and told you everything. And sometimes it was too late by then and they blamed you. My sister who was brought up by an old auntie on our mother's side, she married a second cousin and didn't even know they were related. They don't like that, the old ones; then they blame you.'

'Nanny Ripeka and Dad, they do tell us the old things, every chance they get.'

'Yes, they're fussy about those things. That's why I thought Lena's letter .... Oh I sa-ay. ... But who else? Who else is there?' It was the question I had wanted an answer to, and Auntie Pare was nodding her head, 'Yes, oh I sa-ay, I sa-ay.'

But there were others arriving by now, stamping and shaking the rain off and bringing in armloads of things. 'Not so good this weather for digging.'

'But should clear; the moon will see to it.'

'Sunday is ....'

'Rakaunui.'

I remembered the other time.

Graeme came in the afternoon. For them all to look at and watch, talk to, wonder at, and find out about. At any moment I thought my aunties would begin to poke him to find out what he was made of, to see whether or not he would crumble to a touch.

I was proud of Graeme's quiet friendliness towards my family, and pleased that my family — my aunts and cousins especially — were doing all they could to include him in whatever we did, to make him feel at home.

Sunday was a day as crisp as the new mushrooms that had suddenly appeared, their cawls as yet unsplit. I decided not to go to Nanny Ripeka's to help gather up her kumara. There were enough people to help for the few rows and, as my mother said, you don't tread on an old woman's bunion just to hear her yell.

And it is good to be alone at last with the one you love and who loves you, and who you begin to know and love more and more all the time. We picked the mushrooms and I showed him the trees: Papa Rakau rocking slightly against the new blue wash of sky, and the Leaping Branch, still warm, still smooth, from the touch of stretching fingers, the grasp of fingers clawing, gripping, and hand over hand. Though there was no one now to play there, leaping, stretching, swinging, sliding the long bending fronds.

The ti kouka flowers that had split out in streamers of white at the head of summer had now dried into dark ragged tufts. The round bundles of leaves, which at the tops of the reaching limbs made the tree many-headed, were yellowy and split, and many-eyed from the brown-ridged holes that had formed.

Then in my own tree, which is a quiet tree, we sat on my own branch, still smooth and warm, and talked about the thousands of things, but not the one thing. But I did tell him about the tree and its name. Told him the new name and the old name, and told him the new name which I had chosen for myself because it had seemed important when I was younger to try to be different from the person I was.

The next day we all went to Uncle Rawhiti's to help with his kumara crop so Graeme and I had little more chance to be alone together.

And soon he was gone again. My life became one long wait between letters and week-ends, and holidays when he would get work at the timber yards with Toki. All this time my father was quiet, even friendly towards him, and beginning to treat him like a member of the family. I began to suspect after a while that my father was saving jobs for the week-ends when he knew Graeme and Toki would be there. One week-end it was the roof that needed painting, on another the shed needed repairing or there was weeding or digging to be done. My father was quiet, and different. He seemed tired, so I was glad that Toki and Graeme were there to be the sons he had never had.

And all this time I avoided Nanny Ripeka as much as possible, even though there was something I wanted to say to her, something I wanted to find out.

Then one day my father said to Graeme, 'You love my girl, don't you? You really love her?'

'Yes,' he said. 'I really do.'

'I want you two to get married then.'

14

The days before my wedding were full and busy. And hot, with endless sun that bleached the land of gully and hill, and turned the clay of yet another road to a fine penetrating powder.

'You'll need someone else one day,' my father had said, but I dismissed lightly the small fear that I felt. 'And he has a lot of strength.'

'It's what you wanted.'

'You don't know what it's like yet to be away from here, and from us. And the old lady, she blames me of course, because there's truth in what she says but you have to live a long time ....'

'She's right because she's old?'

'Because she's old she's lived a lot of lives. But you, you'll do right when the right time comes.' I felt the touch of stone but quite warmly.

I hadn't thought about leaving and had perhaps deliberately put these things from my mind. I was happy enough and busy accumulating linen and cutlery, crockery, tea- and coffee-sets. It was important to me then.

And somewhere, I hadn't thought where, there was a house surrounded by flowers, with a lawn to mow and a fence to paint. The inside was a maze of little rooms with soft things on the floor and bright wallpapers and curtains, and furniture from Nanny's magazines. And myself the centre of all this, cooking dishes I'd never tasted or seen before, to amaze my visitors who came and departed constantly.

My mother was anxious that everything should be

right but she enjoyed all the preparation and excitement once the decisions had been made. Each new reply to the gold on white invitation cards that she had sent out in their dozens was a new achievement, a confirmation that all was going well. And that all was as she hoped became more evident as the deep-freeze began to fill with her pies, savouries, and cakes, and the cupboards with preserves of fruit, jars of pickle, and bottles of home-made sauces.

For her own reasons the house had to have a new coat of paint and the flower gardens had to be different from what they'd been before. She had grass growing where there had been flowers, and flowers where there had been lawn, and all this in spite of the dryness of the weather. The drive had a thick layer of new crunching metal.

She had bought herself a new outfit. 'To make me look slim and young.' And skinny shoes 'to make my feet look small like that beauty queen of your father's'. She was enjoying all the organising and the fuss and the new things, and it wasn't until the frocks arrived that I saw her eyes fill.

A few days before the wedding Uncle Bill came with the council bulldozer and scooped two large holes at the back of the section for the hangi, and not long after that Uncle Tom came with firewood on the back of his truck. 'That's the wood, now what about the kai?' my father called. 'What about those pumpkins of yours, Tom?'

'Friday. Friday they'll be cut and ready.'

'And corn?'

'Picking tonight, and Ra and Mereana doing the same. What else, brother? You need any more kumara?'

'No, got plenty. But if you got a spare pig. Running

round. Anywhere ....'

Just then Sonny drove up in the bread van and dropped off four bread crates. 'Hangi baskets,' he said.

'But what about something to go in them? You haven't got a spare pig or two in there, son?'

'No pig, but there's some bread for the stuffing for the pig. Tell Auntie to put plenty of onion in, and plenty of those little bits. You know, those grass clippings. And pepper.'

Later that day Toki came with some short pieces of railway line for the hangi. 'You can't eat those things, son, but if you got a bit of pork ....'

'Save us a trip to the river for stones; they heat up just as good.'

'Next one'll drop off a box of matches to save me rubbing two bits of wood together.'

'You got to admit, Uncle, the match and box is an improvement on the couple of old sticks.'

'You didn't see a pig or two on the side of the road on your way?'

'No luck.'

'Looks like I'll have to go to the butcher.'

The day before the wedding the food began to arrive and soon there wasn't a space anywhere in our house that didn't have boxes or tins containing food. There were bags of potato, kumara, kamokamo, pumpkin, and corn. And, since our freezer had reached capacity long before, my aunties and uncles were relaying pork, chicken, and mutton from freezer to freezer as though they had discovered a new way to play chess. Damp sacks of seafood lined the shed floor and from morning to night the pots simmered and the ovens opened and shut on the great thick wheels of Maori bread. By evening everyone had settled to work the night through.

Everything was going as well as my mother had hoped it would, and yet something was missing and something was wrong.

I went to my room early that night, stepping over the presents they had given. The dinner-set and blankets and bedspreads. Toasters and towels, mirrors, irons, bowls, and tumblers. Heaters, tablecloths, coffee tables.

And stepped under the hanging gown that had caused her eyes to spill. I hadn't been in bed very long when Lena came and got in beside me. 'I'll be sure of a bed and some sleep if I get in now,' she said, and it was comforting to have her there. I asked her what was wrong with everyone but she couldn't or wouldn't answer me.

And the next morning. Still there was something. Something missing and something wrong.

More visitors and more presents, more people laughing and crying. Early fire cracking the already blazing day, and food away in cars to the hall or away in the large baskets ready to be placed over the pits and covered. Flowers in water and last-minute pressing.

Then quite suddenly everyone was gone, leaving me in the beautiful gown that had made my mother cry, feeling sad and not knowing the reason — or knowing but not wanting to know. My father in a new suit, looking miserable, helping me down the path to the car.

The day was trying to be perfect with its stillness and warmth. The sort of day when you could hear Nanny Ripeka's rooster from a mile away over and above the din that the cicadas were making. The sort of day when you could swear that the sky was, after all, solid, and that the few traces of white here and there had been cut and pasted on to it.

Except that there was no time you could have counted trees on a hill on such a day, counted leaves on a tree, counted blades of grass standing some distance away. You could have heard a warm dog snore or a cat walk if there had been a moment to listen.

The sort of day that is supposed to be right for a wedding, that could have right and should have been. I sat quite still in the car, listening to the day's quietness, waiting to know its warmth, waiting for its perfection to flow over me. Waiting and saying nothing, until, when we were almost there, the words came: 'What is it, Dad?' He looked at me but said nothing; then he looked away. 'Stop the car,' I said. Uncle Rawhiti slowed down.

'What's wrong?'

'We're going back. For the old lady.'

'Ah, she won't come.' He'd stopped by now. 'Leave the stubborn old woman where she is.'

'Go back for her; she has to come.'

'We've all talked to her, Baby. She's too old to change.'

'There's something I've got to ask. Go back.'

Uncle Rawhiti turned the car but my father didn't say anything at all.

I ran up the old pathway in the beautiful dress, still clutching the bouquet. 'You've got to come,' I said. She sat there staring at me but didn't say a word.

'Made us turn the car and come for you. ....'

'And there's something I want to know.' Then I began to recite the old names to her, the ones from the wall and the ones before them, and the ones before that. It was strange to hear these old things on the new voice, my voice that had never sounded them before. And if I faltered here and there my father and uncle joined in with me, until I stopped. 'But that's only the trunk of the tree,' I said, 'the length.' And she nodded, waiting for me to go on. 'Now these are the branches that spread everywhere, and I continued the recita- tion, linking every name with every name until there were no more. 'And every branch reaches out,' I said. 'Touches every other.' She nodded again and looked unhappy. 'Who else could there be for me that any of you would have allowed? That there would be nothing against?' 'Not here,' she whispered. 'No one in these parts.' She was crying and holding me close to her, and she was the hill to me, the creek running through, the treasure buried and held fast for all of time. 'Our girl will do right when the right time comes' I could hear my father saying. But I wasn't sure, only sure of one thing just then: 'You have to come.'

'You look very beautiful,'she said. 'Very beautiful.'

'There can be no one else for me, but I can't. Unless you come.'

And after a while she said, 'My clothes, they not ready. I got no hat.'

I threw the bouquet on to the table, ran into the bedroom and took her good frock from the wardrobe. My father was at my feet looking for her shoes so that he could polish them. 'Send Uncle Ra home to get that hat you bought for Mum that she never wore.'

'It's a good hat that. Don't know why she never wears it.'

'It's a kuia's hat. Beside it's too small.'

'Anyone would think your mother had a lot of brains.' He went to tell Uncle Rawhiti where the hat was. I had the iron plugged in and a bath running and I was hunting in a drawer for underclothing.

Nanny looked so good in her best frock and the new black hat that fitted her perfectly. 'Should be you getting married, Old Lady.'

'I told you it was a good hat, but your mother ....'

I snipped a couple of flowers from my bouquet and made a spray to pin on her shoulder. 'There you are. Professional, ay?'

'Ah yes. But your flowers, they might drop to pieces in the church. All those Pakeha will laugh.'

'Never mind. Come on, they'll think our Maori car has blown up.'

Relief on the watching faces as we rounded the corner to the church, and an anxious brushing of jackets, smoothing of skirts and hair. Worried, and watching our arrival, at last. Surprise and tears, seeing her there beside Uncle Rawhiti. Everyone laughing, hugging Nanny, who was skiting about her hat. 'I got my teeth in too, to smile at all the nice people.'

I took my father's arm as the organ sounded. But it wasn't he and I that people saw as they turned to look. It was Uncle Rawhiti bustling Nanny Ripeka to a front seat and my mother rushing suddenly from her place, hugging the old lady, and starting to cry. I wondered briefly what Graeme's family thought at the appearance of so many handkerchiefs. And I wondered if the bouquet would last. I had snipped out the centre-piece and it was all about to collapse.

But now I was beside him. 'She came,' he whispered. Then I was hearing and repeating my name and his. The day had found its perfection after all.

The tables were laid out with salads and cold meats and pickles, and seafoods of every variety, and cakes and sandwiches and savouries. My aunts and cousins in their new hats, feet beginning to know they had new shoes on them, were floating about with large dishes of hangi food held to the level of their chins, so that they all had a strange beheaded appearance. As though through the steam it were their own heads wearing the new hats that were being borne in hot on the dishes, hair done especially for the occasion. Placing the dishes on the tables they became whole again, hurrying out to the kitchen and back with more until it was all done. Then, finding their places at the table, patting moisture from their faces with handkerchiefs.

Uncle Tom said grace, then everything was quiet as we began to eat. Restrained I would say — people wondering how to behave and wondering what to eat and what not to eat. I was noticing and worrying about my mother who wanted everything to be right. And I wondered what the rest of my life would be like. A compromise? Thought of my father saying 'Our girl will do right when the right time comes.' People watched each other not knowing .... My mother leant across to me. 'There was only one thing missing. Now it's here,' she said. And somehow it was like a signal.

The first cork popped as Uncle Rawhiti and the boys who had been serving out hangi came in from the kitchen. 'Don't shoot,' Toki yelled. And all at once people were passing things. Eating — the way my father likes to see. Talking and teasing, yelling and laughing. And my family were looking after Graeme's family, doing everything they could and helping them to make a noise.

Then one by one, first my father, then my uncles, got up to speak, which was not what was on the programme. 'But it's only for show, the programme,' my mother said. 'To make people feel at home.'

Welcoming all, remembering the family living and the family dead, telling some of the old things, some of the new things that had happened since we had all been together last, wishing Graeme and me all the good things. Especially children. I noticed it then — there were no children. Those of my cousins who had children had gone and wouldn't return, and now

103

myself, Lena, the boys, we had grown up too, suddenly …. There were no children at my wedding.

Speaking also of their happiness in knowing the old lady was there. It was a day for handkerchiefs. And for laughing and talking. Singing or chanting the waiata at the conclusion of each speech.

Watching Graeme's family (we were all watching) I noticed a few puzzled expressions and a few puzzled frowns at the programme, but these soon passed as people began to enjoy what I suspect to many was a novelty. And nothing mattered to me at that time except that all was going as my mother and the rest of the family wished. I wanted them to know this, so I went to Toki and told him what I wanted him to say.

The handkerchiefs came out again when he stood, because it was his first time, and my father and uncles called out to encourage him. After he had said all the correct things he spoke about Graeme who was his friend; then he told them what had happened to my tennis racquet and to the clothes the dog had taken away; then he said what I'd asked him to say. And when he finished he began a haka which we all joined in, which could have made the flowers wilt and the walls tumble. I didn't care just then what the rest of my life would be like.

After that we became quiet so that Graeme's family could speak. Two or three of them did and we sang for them. Then Graeme was standing beside me, talking quietly, and especially to my mother and father. And to Toki. Then to his own family who had their handkerchiefs out too. Nothing else mattered just then.

Soon the tables were cleared and folded away and we were all dancing and singing. My feet were knowing the new shoes, as one after the other the men came to dance with me — my father and my uncles, Graeme's father and his uncles, my cousins and his. Now and again we waved to each other as we danced by, and my aunties, two at a time dancing with him, would wave too. Graeme's grandmother was sitting with Auntie Heni and they were both knocking back gins. 'Roll of plastic and a few dry twigs' I heard his grandmother say. 'Myself I like flowers.' My mother and Auntie Mereana were yelling at each other above the din. Their hairdos were coming loose and their shoulder sprays were flattened as though they'd both been smacked. My father was talking to Graeme's mother who was bent double laughing, but holding her drink up so it wouldn't spill; it could have been a new kind of dance. And Toki was dancing cheek to perspiring cheek with someone who had not long arrived, someone I'd never seen before.

Uncle Tom, getting rid of a gate-crasher, then going past yelling to me, 'Bloody jeans, bloody working gear ....' Coming back and going past again, 'Sitting down there large as life boozing ....' Coming past again, 'Never seen him in my life before. Bloody cheek ....' Passing again. 'Just dropped in for a drink he reckoned.' Gone.

And then it was time to leave, saying goodbye with more singing and speeches, hugging, crying, kissing. Sitting down by Nanny Ripeka who had something she wanted me to do. 'What you ask me and what you say, it is right. I been wrong sending my own away from me. You write to your cousin. Tell him come and see this mad old woman before she die. Tell him everything different these days and bring his wife and kids.'

'I'll tell him.'

'And don't you cry. Your eyes will be red and your dress will be spoilt.'

'I'm happy, Nanny.'

'Go on then. And get a baby soon. Before I die.'

15

The day had left a world of navy blue, a warm world of stored sun and pockets of gentle sounds. It was the first time I had been to such a place. Camping had always meant the family and a truckload of belongings at the top of a deserted beach, but now Graeme backed the caravan into the site that we'd been directed to. On one side of us a woman in a sun-dress was trying to get her two children to bed and they were running everywhere in their pyjamas. On the other side an elderly man in shorts who was folding a sun-chair said good evening. I could hear his wife in their caravan scraping a pot.

My mother and father had come home with us while we changed, and Graeme's parents had left to bring the caravan round. It was being lent to us by his aunt. For our honeymoon. I hadn't thought of going away anywhere, hadn't seen, except vaguely amongst the pile of collected items for our 'home', past the day of our wedding. But when Graeme's parents arrived with this little house that was to be ours for a week I felt pleased and excited. So compact and so manageable. So beautiful, hitched at the back of our car, Graeme's and mine. With the little cupboards and drawers, tiny sink and bench, drop table and folding beds.

I felt it could be my home for ever with everything in miniature. Everything within reach so that I was enfolded by the four small walls and the little clothes cupboard and drawer of cutlery, the linen and the pots and pans. The baby fridge in one corner. In another a box containing a child's broom and brush and pan.

Something made me remember the branch where I used to sit alone under the green roof inside the green walls pressing a purple berry or threading necklets of white flowers. I remembered the day not long before, but which seemed long ago, when I had taken Graeme there with me. And we had spoken about our love for one another, with the basket of new mushrooms hanging on a branch above our heads.

My mother too loved the little home on wheels. She excitedly rushed from house to caravan with bottles of preserves, pounds of butter, and loaves of bread. Chicken and hangi food from the hall. Vegetables from the garden. 'Why didn't we have a honeymoon?' she said to my father, running to the house for something else.

'We did.'

'Why not?' she asked on her way back.

'We did.'

'We never' — and she was gone again. 'We never did.'

'We did so.'

'Huh, when? Where did we go for our honeymoon?'

'You should remember' — calling after her. 'I took you down the beach on my motor bike.' It was good to hear them bickering at each other.

I rushed to them and hugged them excitedly, almost like pushing them away. And Graeme's mother and father too. Then we were away, pulling the little house behind us.

'Come on, my wife,' he said, which was another new thing to make me glad. 'Let's eat.' And we spread the cloth, set out what we needed, and sat down to our plates, heaped the way my father would have liked. It was easy to enjoy our first meal alone screened from the pot scraping and child crying and the opening and closing of doors.

And not too difficult later to open the little door and walk away from him to the wash-room and to shower quickly and dress, hoping no one would come. Hoping he would be there waiting so that we would walk back together.

'What's the matter?' he said.

'Nothing. No, nothing.' I took his hand and we walked back slowly.

Safe again inside, with curtains pulled shut, the door closed, and the one globe giving a small warm light. His arms round me, and then holding each other closely and feeling the hardness of him. And knowing this now as part of our love for each other. Glad to feel the tightness in my own body soften under his and happy that I could love him in this way too. Feeling his love and strength deep inside me long after he had fallen asleep. And feeling also the imprint of his body on mine and knowing it was there indelibly. Nothing mattered then but that.

It was easy to step out next morning hand in hand and to walk to the camp store for milk and back again. I opened the windows wide to let the air go through and hooked the door open too. Kids from next door looking in and staring. 'Hallo,' I say, but they don't answer.

'Come out of there,' their mother calls but they don't move. Knocking. Telling us her name. '... off to the beach and it's a lovely day.'

Sorry to leave the little fortress behind, locked up and alone, squatting on its wheels.

And the beach such a public place, like a street, with cars going back and forth and parents pulling children out of the way. Bodies everywhere being massacred by sun but not forgetting the sea. Some hurled themselves at it quite desperately to show why they had come, others stepped timidly, wondering why they had come at all. I was one of these, watching my feet sink into sand and bubbles rise. The sea made of people with only a pretence of water here and there. 'Come on. Come on in.' Thinking of the other place, with its crabbed rocks and ensnared bowls of sky, and its presence of spirits. Where your tread is no more than a shadow, your plunging no more than a ripple.

Flicking water at me and laughing, so that nothing else mattered. Diving at his ankles and he over-balancing. Then away, weaving in and out among the wallowers and gaspers, duckers and divers, floaters and sinkers, and drifters and drowners. Coming after, snatching a foot and losing it, an ankle, losing it, then his hands gripping, holding, and touching quite roughly under the blanket of water. Reaching my own hand out to know him, and wishing my width to be the width of the sea where just then we had our own small place.

So that it was easy walking with him on the sand among the steaming decks of people, and he looking so happy, freckled with drying salt. Far round the beach until there wasn't anyone. Only the two of us, stepping from rock tip to rock tip, then climbing a bank to a hidden place that smelt of summer grass that has the breath of sea on it.

We found many such places during that week. And found in them a deeper and greater love for each other and a greater knowing. But sometimes we would lie on the sea with our finger-tips touching, and I would wonder if it would make sense if, finger-tip to finger-tip, we simply floated away.

16

Looking back on those days, from the time I first met Graeme to the time of the wedding, I know they were happy ones — yet when had my life ever not been happy? I mean that they were exciting times for me in terms of my own hopes and dreams. Only on looking back do I realise that my hopes then were mostly dreams.

My early days had been spent in an enclosure of people and their love, and an enclosure of land and its love — because I've always known that land can love its people and always understood the reciprocity between people and land. But it is not easy to be content with everything that is familiar and safe. My life before I met Graeme was not enough for me, yet I'd lacked the courage to make it different.

And looking back I've asked myself if I did truly love Graeme then, or was he just the means by which I headed towards a dream. And the only answer I've found within myself is that I did love him and that there never could have been anyone else for me. Also looking back I know he had his own dreams too and some of our dreams we shared. We could sit together on a warm gnarled branch and share our dreams and know together the perfection of leaves and the softness of shaded berries. And had we looked up we could have known the greenness of the sky. I did love him. There had never been anyone else to share my tree, not Toki, not Lena, not in the way that Graeme and I shared. This was new. There were other things to share too but not those things which could have shown what might be different between us, remembering the loss of my golden twin, the loss of Margaret.

We arrived back with the caravan to a letter telling of the success of Graeme's application for a new school, spelling out the reality. My dream soon persuaded me that all would be well.

'It's so far away,' I remember saying. 'We don't know anyone.'

'We'll soon know people. It's not so far.'

'Miles.'

'You're not happy?'

'Hadn't thought; it seems so far.' And so final.

'And there's the house.'

So final. No wheels to move it away and back again like the little place that had been ours for a week, now nested on the back lawn as though it might take root and remain there. But I knew better. Soon it would be away again, but without us.

'It'll be ready for us to go into.' Surrounded by flowers, with grass to cut and windows to shine. 'You'll still have me don't forget.'

'No. I'm not. ...'

'And it's not so far ... not too ....'

'... forgetting. And you're right. You *are* right; it's not so far.'

'That's good then.'

'Yes, and the house.'

'Ready for us to move in.'

My parents were pleased when we told them about Graeme's new appointment and about the house that we could have. 'Going away is all right,' my father said. 'As long as you remember. As long as you know where home is and as long as you know all the things we need you to know. Then when the time comes ....'

'The right time.'

'You'll know.'

'And what will I do then?'

'I don't know, but you'll know. You'll do right.'

Graeme must have been more puzzled than I was by what my father said but he didn't ask any questions, and I was glad of this because I wouldn't have known how to answer him. But I noticed that he became quiet. Later he said, 'I love you enough and don't forget that.' I felt reassured by his words.

'I sent the letter,' I said after we had greeted her. And she handed me a telegram. It was from Hemi to say that he would be coming to stay with her at Easter. 'And I got some pots for you,' she said. 'For your wedding present. Some for you, some for your cousin when he comes. Come and see which pots you want.

She took us into the sitting room where she had the sets of saucepans displayed quite grandly on the side-board. I could tell she was pleased. I chose. 'You and your boy stay with me tonight. I got our tea on.'

While we were eating Nanny said, 'If my son say this boy all right for his girl then I trust my son. Doesn't matter if it's a Pakeha or not.' I knew it was no use trying to stop Nanny saying what she would say. I tried not to mind and hoped Graeme wouldn't feel too uncomfortable. 'But your Nanny, she's not all wrong. She's old but she not all wrong.'

'I know, Nanny.'

'But wrong to blame you and wrong to send your cousin away.'

'It's all right. Everything's all right now. ...'

'This boy, he got to go your way now. Otherwise there will be nothing. Because you have to have someone to get your children with, even if it's a Pakeha. Never mind, this silly old kuia will have every-

thing right before she die. You like my kai, boy?'
eyeing him with her two gimlets. He nodded. 'A
good-looking boy,' she said, pleased about how
Graeme was enjoying the food and helping himself to
more. 'A good-looking boy and strong. You will get
good babies with my grand-daughter, good-looking
and strong.' There was nothing for Graeme to say; he
was quiet and perhaps wondering how he was going to
see a night through at Nanny's place.

Later we picked a few flowers and went to be with
Grandpa Toki and the others for a while, and I wanted
to tell Graeme about what had occurred on the night
old Toki died. It would have been right to tell him
then under the stillness of the hills by the quiet of the
creek, but I didn't. I should have told him too what we
had found once near there, and what had happened
later, and what it meant to me. But I couldn't. We
went back into the house bringing the wood in for
morning.

'There's your bed,' Nanny said, with her old eyes
sparking mischief. 'Never you worry, Ripeka, never
you worry, boy. It don't squeak.'

And during that week before it was time to leave I
noticed that my mother and father were pushing
Graeme and me towards each other all the time.

'You must be tired,' my mother would hint, even if it
was only three o'clock in the afternoon. 'Yes, you
better go and have a lie down,' my father would say.

'I'm not tired, Dad, I've done nothing but eat and
sleep.'

'Gee, some people are dumb' — beginning to shout.
'Don't you want to be alone with your husband?'

'Yes, but we were going to watch telly for a while.'

My father would get a look of despair, 'Well, I want
a grandson out of you two before I'm much older. But
you two better have plenty of practice first.' Aue! But it

113

was because they wanted to know that we were all right and happy, wanted our love for each other to be evident before we went from there.

17

The city was a great loom weaving its tangles and tufts of people into haphazard multicoloured fabric.

We shuttled outward from the knot of parked cars and found ourselves hand in hand in the moving threads travelling back and forth the length of the main shopping centre.

People, so many of them. Some clutching their clothing about them and hugging bags as though all could suddenly be snatched away. Knowing where they were going and what they were doing, leaning into each headlong step. Some strolled, as though there was nowhere at all to go, nothing whatever to do, only walking, and eating sometimes from an oily paper bag.

We two went hand in hand eagerly round and about the red sale flags and the tide of signs announcing Bargains and Bus Stop, Self Help, Red Band, Beauty Parlour, P5, Hot Pies, Cross Now. And warning No Smoking and No Bread, Wait, No Dogs, Don't Spit, Do Not Remove From Shelves.

Excitedly we went, with a parcel of curtain material and a packet of needles and pins, bought from a pink woman with blue hair and crabby knuckles. Thumped the rolls we had chosen on to the counter and tumbled out the rippling lengths. Warped fingers swooping with scissors, tossing the stuff into folds again and again.

It was easy to be pleased and excited hand in hand in the warp and weft of the city, with its stores and sales and sights and smells, its people leaning into the long streets. And some of them barefooted. Some wearing blankets. Some carrying their babies on their backs. I wondered what my mother would have made of that.

Then back to the house that was nothing like the dream after all. No flowers, no fences to need painting, only a scabby lawn and a few cobwebbed thistles leaning across a disintegrating pathway — and the house. It was good to know that it didn't matter after all, and it was exciting and different to peer through the bubbled glass as we fitted the key when we'd first arrived. Into the empty rooms, seeing them as they could be, opening the windows and letting the warm air in. We sat on the floor waiting for the rest of our things, and the house had the right feeling. There was no threat — then — from the bare walls and empty corners or from the inward unblinking eyes that were the windows. The house seemed to accept us as we sat on the warm boards waiting for the van to come.

And when it did arrive at last there were the bed and dressing-table that my mother and father had given us, and the table and chairs from Graeme's parents, boxes of kitchenware and crockery and linen and blankets. There were cupboards and drawers to be washed. Packing, sorting, a few decisions to be made. We worked well into the night putting everything into place, and I don't know about Graeme but I worked quite happily

And not far away, just over the next hill, the city opened out like a gigantic flower. How I wanted to hold it in my hand.

'So we are here,' I wrote, 'settling into our first (should I say second?) home together. We have about us all the nice things that everyone gave and we are both very happy.

'The house. Sits on a hillside, is painted a dull blue, and has two bedrooms. It is small and tidy and quite comfortable. The ground here looks hard and dry.

'We went down to the city this morning. An exciting place. Buildings so gigantic that walking among them you feel the world has suddenly become skyless. Without sky. Even though you glimpse a little of it now and again if you think of looking up. And so much to see, so many beautiful things to buy, I know you would like it here. I know Nanny would love to look at all the furniture and all the rugs and drapes that are on display. But your feet would get sore like mine did.

'On the way back from town we called in at the post office to fill in an application for a telephone so don't be surprised if you get a phone call one of these days. I miss you all but not too much, and you'll have to tell everyone at home to write to me.

'Curtain material, that's what we went to town for. And cotton and pins, and a packet of needles and a big pair of dressmaker scissors. ("Dressmaker scissors", that's what it had on the label.) I have to sew them by hand, the curtains, but I don't mind. It's something I enjoy doing even though I'm impatient to have them finished.

'Graeme goes back to school next week but I don't think I'll mind being on my own because I've made all sorts of plans and know I'll be busy.

'Didn't finish describing the house to you but hope you'll come and see us soon. Easter? And you'll be able to see for yourselves, and we'll have all sorts of things to talk about. The house, it's not much different from any other in the street. Funny not knowing the names of people living next door and across the road. No, not much different and it seems all right. I had a strange dream last night, about the house.'

'We have shown your letter to everybody' my mother wrote. 'Nanny Lena Toki Uncle Tom and Auntie Heni and the boys and Auntie Mereana and Uncle Ra when they came down the week-end. Their farm is doing good this year. We are pleased how you have both settled in and knowing about the house too. And the town with all its good things. Graeme's Mum and Dad came over Sunday to get the caravan and they stay the afternoon with us. They said they have a letter too from you both.

'Well it's quite lonely here now you two are gone and everybody gone since after the wedding. But never mind we know you two are happy.

'I'm telling Dad to come there at Eastertime but he is saying it is time for the gardens which is right. But I said never mind the gardens because they are not so big this year. There's enough younger ones here to dig. I think he agrees with me and I think we will come. And Lena said she'll come with us.

'Tomorrow I will get the prints from the wedding so we can order all our photos and I will send them to you so you two can have a look and order some too. Well I'm really looking forward to seeing how they turn out.

'Never mind ringing up when you get your phone on because it cost too much. And Dad said don't think too much about your dreams. Everyone is well and send their love to both of you.'

They were good days. Days of full sun which scorched the section a light biscuit colour and set blisters erupting in the softening asphalt of the roads and foot-paths. Days for talking and planning, for listening to words of our dreams and watching them float about us in all their changing colours.

And when Graeme went back to school I planned to be too busy to feel his absence, because there was the

118

house to look after and all our new things to care for. And there was shopping too, although not as much as I'd expected. And not as much cooking either, but I liked to try new things and to see everything looking good and almost touching the dream.

It was a quiet street with scarcely a movement and there was time once he'd gone to notice the quiet and the stillness. Somewhere beyond the next hill teams of people worked the great machine that was the city, oiling every cog, screwing every nut down tight. But here there was only the tinkle of tricycles, the slamming of a door, the occasional knock of heels on concrete and asphalt.

Then, later, Graeme would come with news of all he'd done, with a heap of books to mark, looking happy because I was there. He showed me how to mark the books and sometimes he would bring home a typewriter and ask me to type something for him. I was pleased to be helpful, loved the bright sheet of paper that I turned in under the roller, and the print running on to the page at the tapping of my fingers. I could be happy then. Sometimes there was a stencil to cut. And there was a small bottle of fluid in case I made a mistake but I hardly used it. 'Not bad for a Maori' I'd say as I handed him the work. And I knew he didn't like me saying that, but I said it to tease him, and to tease myself a little too, because of all the strange thoughts I had, and all the strange feelings.

Sometimes after our evening meal if Graeme didn't have too much to do we'd go down to see a film, or on late shopping nights we'd go into the city and I'd buy little things for the house.

On the day that the phone was connected I rang through, waiting long enough to make sure my father would be back from work. Before I spoke I could hear my mother on the other end calling, 'Come quick,

quick. It's Ripeka.' She had forgotten the name I'd given myself. 'Hallo, Ripeka,' she yelled in my ear. I could have cried for the closeness of her.

Then I talked excitedly about all the good things, then I spoke to my father and told him all the same things too. I didn't mention the strange thoughts, the strange feelings I sometimes had. I wanted them to be assured that I was all right, and in this I was taking my cue from my father who had told me not to think too much about my dreams. I got Graeme to come and talk to them for a while, then I took over again. 'Be sure to bring some of your bread. At Easter. And some of your fruit-cake. When you come at Easter.' Bring this, bring that. 'Bring some mussels for Graeme and me.'

'What about your mother? If we bring all those things there'll be no room for your mother. She's not too small.'

'Stick her on top of everything. And bring Lena ....'

'Get off that phone,' I could hear her yelling. 'Stop talking and wasting all our Baby's money. You better pay her phone bill when you get there.'

I put the receiver down and felt the tears rushing but I brushed them off and made a cup of tea for Graeme and me. I couldn't say anything. 'What's this?' he said. 'Chocolate cake!' He was being good to me. 'That's what I like. Cut a whole quarter and put it on a plate for me.'

So I did. I cut myself a small slice too and felt it crumble down my throat and stick there.

I had told them the good things, but not the one thing that had begun to puzzle and frighten me. Not the one thing that I felt only they would know about.

There was Graeme, so quiet, so good to me always. But I would not have told him of these thoughts and feelings even if they had been tangible enough to

express at that stage. I had never forgotten my friend-
ship with Margaret, how close we had once been, and I
thought often about the things only she and I had
shared. Then suddenly one day I didn't know her, and
I was afraid this could happen again. I hadn't seen
her since that day.

I remembered too the conversation in Grandpa
Toki's kitchen when we'd brought home the stone,
when I discovered that in some things there can be no
bridge to understanding.

So there were some things, I thought, I could not
speak about to Graeme — not then. Not until it was
almost too late did I find that completeness of understanding is not so important when there is love.

My father, I had begun to realise too, had agreed to
my marriage to Graeme because he had brought about
a change in himself. He had always, although he did
not express it in words, seen our home and the family
land as a spiritual sanctuary, a kind of stronghold for
all of us. But, then he had begun to hope, if I moved
away from there into what he thought of as a Pakeha
world, I should find a second sanctuary. He had begun
to see Graeme as the central part of this second
sanctuary, as someone who would be strong, who
would help and protect me. I would not, as my father
saw it, exchange our old way of life for the new way but
would learn to be part of both, as I had already begun
trying to be some years before.

The stone was my inheritance. It would always be
so, but he wanted me to have another inheritance as
well. And he would have been thinking too of the
children that Graeme and I would have who would
inherit both ways of life.

18

During Easter week a van arrived with our new television set. We had decided on it one late shopping night. Something else for me to dust and polish and fuss over. I was pleased with the way the dark wood glowed under my rubbing.

And I thought to myself that after Easter I could get work in an office somewhere in town, then we could have all sorts of things for the house, and perhaps then ....

Wondered what it would be like working in a strange place where I didn't know anyone. The idea scared me a little but the more I thought about it the more sure I was that it would be good for me to have work. We needed things. To fill the corners and for me to clean and polish, things to crowd out the strangeness I now so often felt. And with work I could be away from the house. ... I wondered if they would notice when they came at Easter, the strangeness, the faint scentiness that all my rubbing and scrubbing could not dispel.

It was a relief to see at last the old car, packed to the windows, stopping outside our place, and my mother in a new dress getting out and looking really good. My father in his wedding shirt, looking about him, wondering what sort of place this was his daughter was living in. Then Lena.

I ran to my mother and held her closely, then to my father, then Lena. And Graeme bundled their rolled up mattress out of the back seat and took it inside.

But after Easter I was feeling too unwell to think of looking in the paper or going out to work. I was tired after all the late nights, being together and getting all the news. And from driving about with them showing them the city. I went to bed after they'd gone and was still sleeping when Graeme left for school the next day.

At mid-morning I put my feet to the floor and felt it swoop beneath me. So I got back into bed and was soon asleep again.

'You're not well.'

'You're home.'

'It's nearly five. You're not ....'

'Our baby.' I said it not caring, only stumbling into the bathroom to be sick, and he hovering and not knowing what to do or how to feel. 'Get you to the doctor,' I could hear him saying, 'tomorrow. You're pleased ... are you?' I don't think I answered. 'Or will you be, when you feel better?' I may have nodded but perhaps I didn't. 'Please don't be ill, my darling.' He got into bed with me and held me closely to him.

The next morning I woke with a dry throat, my head was aching, and he was beside the bed with a cup of tea. 'Yes, I'm pleased. Will be ....'

'And I'm cooking you some breakfast because you'll have to eat.' (Have a *good* breakfast.) 'Your mother was right; you've lost so much weight and got little enough to lose.'

'My girl,' she'd said, 'you'll have to get a bit of beef on you. Look at you, your eyes are dropping out.' And then quietly she'd asked if something was wrong. But I hadn't wanted to tell her of my fears, which seemed anyway to have diminished now that my family were there.

My father had spoken to me too. I could only know by living in a place, he'd said, whether it was all right or not. 'At home we know where everything is; in a place like this there's no telling. Only time and how you are affected will tell.'

'I have Graeme,' I'd said.

'Yes, but perhaps I was wrong thinking he would be enough protection; perhaps I was wrong thinking you could be different in a different place.'

'No no, you weren't wrong,' I said — because I didn't want him to be wrong.

'You don't seem well,' he said.

'I've been working hard about the house, forgetting to eat. No Dad here to make me eat.'

'Well, you look after yourself a bit better, Baby, and stay on for a while. If it's no good for you here then find another place, come home for a time if you have to. But I don't want to say too much to you. I don't want you to dwell on these things which can be so worrying.'

'I've got a new life now and I can put all of these old things out of my mind. ....'

'But that could be wrong. Your Nanny would say it's wrong to do that.'

I was not used to indecision from my father and it made me sad. 'If anything's wrong,' I said, 'I'll let you know once I'm sure. We'll move away.'

'You won't fight against it for too long?'

'I won't.'

We didn't speak of these things again.

I picked at the breakfast Graeme brought me, then got up to be sick again.

'I'll ring at lunch-time to see how you are, and I'll be home early to get you to the doctor.' He looked worried and unhappy. I asked him to lock the doors for me; then I turned the pillow to its cool side and drowsed again.

'It will pass,' the doctor said. He took my weight, prescribed iron, and told me what I should eat. 'Come back in a month. And make an appointment at the clinic. Go there. Ask for her.' He wrote a name on a card. 'Don't smoke,' he said.

I decided not to make the appointments — the doctor had said himself that it would pass. And it was not the baby or the sick feeling that worried me.

'Your father will be pleased.'

'And Mum and the others.'

'You could ring through.'

'Yes, tonight.'

'And I'll drop my mother and the old man a line. I can just see Gran. ... You're pleased, Linda? You're all right?'

'Yes, I'll be all right. I can't wait for our baby.'

The dreams had in them a tall woman with moko on her chin, a woman I didn't know, who beckoned from the corner of a room. A strange room. Beckoned me to come to her, but I knew I must not move. I knew not to go with her.

'Don't think too much about your dreams' my father had said. Soon I would write and tell them how afraid I often felt, how I busied myself all day long to stop myself from thinking, to arrest the feelings I had.

'And you mustn't overdo things; there's no need,' Graeme said.

'Like to be busy, need to, until you come home.'

'No need. You should rest more. Lie down and have a quiet read. You always like to read.'

'Can't settle to it.' — Not with the cold that comes in.

'But you'll try?'

'Yes.' — And the dreams more and more real.

125

'I've got to look after you.'

'I'll try.'

'And got to look after our baby too.'

'It's good having a baby to look forward to.'

Soon I would write to my parents and tell them how frightened I was and how ill I felt. I would tell them there was something wrong in the house and that I couldn't fight against it any longer. There was no protection from it.

I had promised my father that I wouldn't wait too long, but I didn't write to my parents for some time. I wrote instead to Nanny Ripeka and to Lena and my other cousins, but writing only the good things and asking each of them to come and stay even though I knew they couldn't. Wrote a letter each day, slowly and carefully, to help the time pass, penning each comma perfectly and putting each stamp carefully in place on the envelopes.

Each day I posted one of the letters, glad to be away from the house that I had begun to dread. Dawdling along the quiet street, and sorry to see each letter drop and know it was time to return. Sorry most especially to see the last one go, to hear it slide and shuffle into the bundle as though it were nothing after all. Knowing there was one more letter to be written but I wouldn't write it, not yet.

Then returning, going inside, I felt strongly and certainly the iced touch, the chill pricking across my shoulders and head and down my back — and I blocked the welling scream with my hand.

Went out then, locking the door behind me, and walked the streets until it was time for Graeme to come home.

'What's wrong? Where have you been?'

'Just walking.' Because how explain the chilled

fingers on my neck, stroking the length of my spine.
The icy grip on my arms and legs, taking me away.

'You look so tired, my love, and so thin. So unwell.'

'Walking. Here and there.'

'Instead of resting. You won't rest, won't go back to
the doctor?'

'It'll do me no good. There's nothing he can do.'

'I'll take you tomorrow.'

'There's nothing, it's nothing to do with that.'

'What do you mean?'

'I can't have the baby here. Not here. A baby can't
live here. I'll have to go home. ...'

'But this is home, Linda. This is home now.' Home?
It was difficult to understand how Graeme could think
of this as home.

'Why don't you trust me?' he said. 'Why won't you
tell me?'

I had never seen him look so unhappy. But how
could I say anything to him? I checked the tears that
were brimming, only to feel them, quite suddenly,
cascading down inside me.

The next morning as soon as he had left I sat down to
write to my mother. I wrote hurriedly, not looking
about, my teeth biting into my hand to prevent the
scream. Then went out, locking the door.

At the corner I dropped the letter into the box and
felt my trembling legs moving me down the hill to the
bus stop.

There was a grey cold in the city, with a pinching
wind hooping fragments of the day along the grooves
of road. I was thankful for the bowling litter — the
chip cartons and ice-block wraps, the screwed bags,
used tickets and dockets and take-away papers. And
for the kicked bits of pie, the cigarette ends, and the
wads of tooth-marked gum. That showed that people
lived.

Smells too to be thankful for. Pub and urine stink, and the cloying smells of the delicatessen. The sweat smells and the antiseptic, the cooking and must, the musk, the coffee, the waste flesh burning.

And the noises. Wooden footfalls of the hundreds of wooden people and their unheard crying. Vehicles shifting and stopping, packing, unloading. The building, the breaking, the selling and buying.

People. Moving about among the debris, the smells, and the noise. Tramping forever the beaten pavements, pale and staring; sitting sometimes inside the jostling cars and buses, framed by squares of glass.

Sometimes I saw my cousins among the people but they didn't recognise me. Sometimes I saw Mum and Dad or my old Nanny from back home. Or my Auntie Rangi with a parcel under her arm — but she lived far away from here. I would follow them for a while, only to find that they were strangers, so I would turn back and search the faces again.

Each day I went, striding thankfully the littered loud streets, and returned when it was time for him to come home, hoping that he wouldn't know or wouldn't ask — because what could I say?

At last one afternoon the letter was there.

'... I'm coming to stay with you until you are well and until we can move you from there because these are old matters. We want you to come home but it wouldn't be right for you to leave your husband who is a good husband to you and we know he loves you very much. And it wouldn't be right to make him bring you back here to live unless he has to. Because it would not be good for him and it would make him different. He needs to be his own and to have you beside him and that would be too hard for him here. Your father and I are too close to you and he would suffer inside him.

'We took your letter to Nanny and read it to her and she said go there to you because you are ill and these are old matters. And that's the first thing your father and I thought of too when we read your letter. But you know it yourself. You miss us too and that makes it worse but that is not all there is. Because your father wondered when he was there at Eastertime. These are old concerns and we would have to go back a long way to know exactly. But where you are is a bad place for you. It must be a burying place for this to happen. It should be left to those who were there first and it is no place for you.

'So I am coming but I don't want your Dad to come because these things affect him after a while but not me so much. And he is not well already. Also someone has to look after this place here because I won't leave you until I know you are all right again. And that will take time. You and Graeme will have to get another place to live very soon and you will have to make him understand this. It would be very bad for your baby and you.

'I have taken a few days to answer your letter and I'm sorry because you must have been very unhappy and waiting but we have been talking it all over and trying to do what is best.

'You have to tell Graeme everything and trust him. He might not understand but I think he will do what you want because he loves you. You have to tell him all the things you had in your letter to us and all the other things you have never spoken about. You've never spoken about them because you think your roots are too far apart yours and his and will never touch. That is what you are scared to find out but you have to be brave. You love him and you're scared to find out that underneath you and him are far apart and far different. More than you want to think but he loves you and will do his best.

'When you two have talked deeply enough then you will know. Bad or good. If you two find out that you can never touch in the deep things of the spirit because of what you have deep in you then you will have to come back to us. Because you will get too weak and so will he. But if you two find out that you can reach out far enough to each other then you have to be brave enough and stay. You have been doing your best to go towards him but you have not allowed him to come towards you and it is not his fault. You keep things to yourself because you think he will not understand. And perhaps he won't but you'll soon know. And we need you to be what you are and that's important. And we need you to hold on to what is in you.

'I could bring old Toka with me if he was here but he is away for some weeks down south and we can't wait for him. He could come with me and give his advice and perhaps do your house to make it safe. As you know this is his work. But I think he would say no leave it to those there before. He's the one we've always gone to with these matters. To send spirits on their way. But this was family. It was family matters. This time we know nothing about it so it's much better for you to go. That's important. But I'll come until you've talked to each other. Until you find somewhere.

'This is a very long letter but I've still got more to put. I will tell you what we didn't tell you before. Dad didn't want you to go away from us. Because you are still young in many ways. And also we need our people here especially the ones who have been taught family things. And he would have told you to wait longer. But he has been sick and you noticed yourself how quiet he was but he tried to hide it. He got to like Graeme and to trust him and I think you were surprised. But

Graeme is right for you and your father knows he loves you and it goes deep. Because we won't be here forever him and I. Then what would you do. So he wanted to see you settled and safe. He went against Nanny's wishes letting you marry Graeme which was very hard for him to do. And hard for me too but it turned out good we think.

'Now when we got this letter from you he is so upset. We have both cried for you but it's no use crying any longer. Everything will have to be all right for you one way or the other. You might stay or you might come home to us if Graeme cannot agree you should find another place but I'm sure he will.

'You have to explain everything to him so you two can move away from there very soon. But it takes time. And that is why I have to come so you will not be alone because alone it will get to you much easier. That's what your grandmother said and I believe her.'

I hid the letter away because how could I tell him? How could I let him know what my mother's letter said?

'She's coming tomorrow,' I said the night before.

'How do you know?' And his voice was far away.

'I had a letter.'

'You didn't tell me.' Far away yet angry.

'It's ... somewhere. I've put it somewhere.' Because how could I show him what it said.

'Well, that should stop you roaming about the place every day.' We were far apart he and I. 'Just as well she's coming; she might be able to talk some sense into you. ...' Because Nanny Ripeka was right after all.

19

The room trembled, undulated, as though it were on the sea going somewhere far away. And in the undulating room the bed I lay on had elongated, the foot lengthening until it was out of sight, disappearing into a point of darkness. Then the darkness itself grew, grew until it was all-pervading and I knew I had to go. I knew I must begin a long journey into the darkness, because somewhere in that darkness someone unseen beckoned.

And an unheard voice called.

It was a road now. The darkness was an unending road where every step must be trod carefully because I could not see. Hands searching the darkness for something to touch, held out for someone to take, but there was nothing to touch and no one to guide me.

Unable to turn back because a voice called though it couldn't be heard, an arm beckoned but remained unseen. Groping with nothing before me, stumbling along a road that had now lost all solidity, a dark way without substance. A stretch of night that was endless.

And then a white stab of light in the distance. A speck growing as I walked towards it. Growing and growing, diminishing the dark until all was illuminated.

Now seeing everywhere and everything. I was at the edge of a cliff. Standing looking out over a crashing white sea.

Over the sea a white owl swooped, its eyes burning white.

And I could leap out of the light into the burnished sea to meet the darkness again, the darkness which was age-long, the imperishable darkness, the darkness for ever and unending.

I could. But then the swooping owl flew close by and it knew me. I thought I heard my name as it settled away from me. Fluorescent on an illuminated rock. Then white rock and white bird merged. Merged and changed. They had become a woman, and I heard my name quite clearly now, saw the great arm beckon.

So I turned away from the curdling sea and its reaching darkness and went towards her, her eyes white fire, her chin intricately scrolled. She reached out and held my shoulders quite lightly, though I was sure I did not know her, did not belong to her. Our noses pressed. Once. An intake of breath between us. Then again.

Then her face was growing. Swelling. And her great nose pressing harder and harder. Her swelling hands crushed my shoulders. Clamping my face to hers. And I opened my mouth to scream, to cry, but no sound came.

'I'm here.' I heard her voice as from far away. 'Always here. ...' And she was by me, holding me closely.

'Don't let me sleep.'

'You're tired, very tired.'

'The dream.'

'You must go against them ... no matter who wants you. No matter who calls you in your dreams you musn't go. And remember that I'm here. All the time. But I must get you away. You'll have to talk to Graeme.'

'But not yet.'

'Yes, now. Or I will.'

'Couldn't we just go?'

'It wouldn't be right.'

'You and I?'

'Only if we have to after you've spoken to him. Let me do it for you.'

'No, no. I will. Tonight when he comes home ....' Because there was something I had to tell him. Something. But how could I ... if I couldn't remember. I wondered what it was I'd been going to say.

'As soon as he comes home.' Who? Wondered who it was we were talking about, and why I was there in that house. Somewhere and nowhere at all. 'Let's go out. Walk for a while.'

'All right. But not too far. To the corner and back.' To keep from sleeping. Must never sleep again — or perhaps it would be easier, after all, to sleep.

And not long after that he was home, coming up the path with an armload of books. And my mother was talking to him as though he was someone she knew, someone close to her. She was setting the table and putting food on to the plates. I tried to eat and thought that after I'd eaten I would go to bed to sleep. It would be better and easier just to sleep.

But she was helping me up from the table and telling me to do what I had to.

'I can't. I've forgotten ....'

'You haven't forgotten,' she said, and not speaking gently to me.

'Nanny Ripeka was right.'

'Don't think of her now. Think of yourself and your baby, and your husband ....'

'I don't know him; he doesn't know me. Love is what you know.'

'I know you,' he said, coming towards me. I had forgotten he was there. 'You're my wife. And this is our child.' He put out a hand to touch the baby that bumped about inside me like a trapped bird. Only the baby seemed real.

The other weight did not stir, but remained like rock inside me.

'Something's gone wrong, but I do love you. We can make it right again, if only I can know.'

'I'm so tired and I need to sleep.'

'Later,' she said. 'When you've said all there is. Or I'll do it for you.'

'I would. I will, when I remember ....'

'The main thing is to get away. From here.' She was looking at him. Telling him. 'Get her away.'

'Remember how we used to drive about in the car together?' He was speaking to me.

'Long ago.'

'Talking.'

'Such a long time ago.'

'We'll do that now.'

'Away from here there's nothing to be afraid of,' she said.

'In the car until everything's said. We can drive all night if we need to and you can talk to me. Tell me all there is.'

'Go,' she said.

'I can't remember.'

'You can remember, and the letter will help.' I put my hand to my pocket. I'd had her letter with me ever since I received it, to keep me from forgetting. 'Come with us then, you can't stay here,' I said.

'I think I'll stay. Pack a few things. I'll be all right. Go now.'

We didn't speak, driving the darkened roads, slowing and stopping for the lights. Amber and red, and the motor revving. Green. People, only a few, walking the pavements with hands pocketed. All thin people, the night's people, faces stung by the night's cold and yellowed by the sallow lighting of the streets.

For minutes or hours we didn't speak, yet I did remember as he reached out and moved me close to him. Away from there I could remember what it was I had to say. 'I'll always love you,' he said, after minutes or hours. 'And I you,' I said. 'And there would never be anyone else for me — will never be.' So after a while, after minutes but not hours, he said, 'Are you leaving me?'

'No, not leaving, not unless you think there's no other way. But there were times, bad times, when I knew it would be easier than saying ....'

'But there's nothing. Is there? That could be so difficult to say.'

'It's not the saying. Only the finding out.'

'Tell me.'

'About you and me. That we don't know each other after all, that we never can. Afraid that our differences are too great.'

'Yet we've never had big differences.'

'There are things. Things I've never said because I've felt there couldn't ....'

'Be understanding?'

'Understanding and knowing — and that without these we would be strangers.'

'Because love is what you know?'

'Sometimes I have the feeling of belonging to a different time, and I'm sure, quite sure, part of me does.'

'And now you're beginning to tell me. Tell me without any worry, my love. Because, after all, we can know ....'

'Without understanding?' Like we know darkness and the wind and the lulling of sun. Like we know shadowed pathways and fresh or fetid smells that come from the earth, sting of berries crushed to a mauve pulp, know that you love a person, know the vigour of the unborn. Like knowing about the commitment between sky and earth, and the commitment between earth and people.

'I need to move from there.'

'But not leaving.'

'The house. Only the house.'

'Only the house. Then it's all right and it's settled. We won't go back.' And we were both silent, moving so slowly along in the darkness, which was not a real darkness now but simply a warm blanket of night which would eventually peel itself back on a breathing daylight.

Thinking about what he had just said I knew the extent of his love for me and the extent of mine for him. 'Now you can tell me.'

'All the recent things first, and then the other things.'

So then I told him, a fusion, perhaps a confusion, of past things and what was happening to me then, and why.

The streets were emptying and I was like those emptying streets as I spoke about my whole life, and about what was in me that was buried and unchangeable and significant. Talking on and on as we drove — until there was nothing more. 'We'll go back now and get her,' he said. 'You're the one to know you're right and it's not for me to question what you know. Don't you see?' We had stopped in the dead still of darkness, holding each other and knowing the warmth of the dark all about. 'It shouldn't be too late to book in somewhere but if it is we'll just wait in the car until morning.'

Back towards the city, the headlights cleaving the night like two machetes, and no one.

137

No one. A piece of paper, or a white bird perhaps, lifted on a soft gust, and the two of us riding silently the emptied roads.

20

There were two rooms at the top of a noisy flight of stairs, voices billowing up from below, hollowed by the funnel that was the stairway. Cisterns and exploding doors, and always someone's music syncopated by drops of water from loose-necked taps.

It was a place for noise yet it was quiet.

And looking out and down through the jammed window — the big window made of little windows — I could see traffic sidling past a hole in the ground. Past canvas and drums and lamps and flags where the men at work pick-axed rock and lifted slabs of road with juddering drills and heaved shovelfuls of sludge and stone on to wet yellow-bright heaps.

Feet rapped the patchworks of asphalt all day and most of the night, and sometimes at night a baby somewhere cried, and someone blew tousled sounds from a muted saxophone. A place for noises and for smells too.

Layer upon layer of smells from those who had come and gone — who were all the time coming and going. Each had left his own stink on the stairs, his own cooking taints on the eroding walls and ceilings, pervading corners and cupboards and cracks. From outside, the Take Away gave off its heating oils and brewed coffee, batter and fish-frying.

'Not what I wanted. Not what I'd hoped for,' he said.

'But it's all right, I know it's all right.'

'It's quiet,' she said.

'All I could get in a hurry, but we'll find something
....'

'Where I can turn round without knocking someone
over.'

'Where we won't get a mouthful of plaster every time
we snore.'

'Where you don't have to shout to hear each other.'

'But it's a quiet place; it'll do for now.'

'As long as you're all right, Baby,' my father said.
'That's the main thing. You don't have to worry about
your tough old Dad. Come on now, no more crying.'
Yet it was a relief to cry. Over all the hours and weeks I
hadn't once cried, not even when my mother arrived.
So some of the tears were for myself.

'But you look so tired, so thin ....'

'No more. Or I'll have to hang my shirt out on the
line to dry. Where do you ...? I don't see no clothes-
line here. Anywhere?'

'There are more stairs, going out the back.'

'Besides your puku's getting in the way. You might
knock me over and Mum'll get wild. Ay, Mum?'

'Arriving so unexpectedly, and looking so skinny and
tired ....'

'And anyway go and kiss your cousin.'

Shuffling at the top of the stairs, a mattress coming
in through the open door — 'Toki!'

'My cuzzy. How's my cuzzy? Just as black as ever?'

'Just as black, yes. And fatter.'

'That'll wear off.' I could feel his tears on my face.
'The puku will wear off, as long as the black don't.'

'Won't, and can't.'

'I had to come.'

'I know.' He went to my mother and then to
Graeme. 'And anyway I couldn't let the old man come
on his own; look at him.'

140

'We'll have to do something about my Dad.'

'You've got a few days off both of you?' my mother asked.

'I have,' my father said. 'But our nephew here, he's got off permanent.'

'The sack?'

'Took a week off to settle some affairs.'

'Romantic affairs.'

'The girl at our wedding?'

'That's the one. We met when I was away that time. Had to go far afield to find me the right girl.'

'The right girl?'

'We're getting hitched up.'

'Married? I'm really happy for you. ... Mum!'

'I heard. Come here, boy,' she said, putting her arms out to him. 'We're all happy for you.'

'And I'm happy for me too. No job though. Came back after the week away and told my boss about the big romance and all that. And he was a bit grumpy but he took it okay, didn't sack me ....'

'Then he took another day off and went to the beach,' my father said.

'Well, I went over to see my uncle here to tell him about me and my girl and I saw him looking like this. So I took the next day off to get some kai for him because I knew there would be a good tide. Then I got back and we had a feed and the next day I went back to work and I got my marching orders.'

'Well, that's good anyhow, that means you could come and see us.'

'Anyway I had to. Needed to know — same as him. And now I'm here I can get some free advice from my mate, now I'm going to be a married man.'

'You brought us some kai of course?'

'Would we come with our bellies full and our hands swinging? I'll get it from the car.'

I was happy hearing the shuttle of shell as Toki and Graeme lowered the wet bag on to newspaper in the kitchen, and I remembered that for a few years I had scorned these foods that were now more than sustenance to me. I pressed the two halves of a spiny shell apart and very gently worked a sliver away from the inside. I put it on my tongue, and the crushed-bitter taste permeated my mouth. My fingers were stained darkly with the deep red of the juices. And soon the potful of mussels began to heat and the shells to open slowly in the grey frothy water coming to the boil, revealing the cream-coloured flesh with the edgings of black rind. Loosening from the shell and pulling the tufts away: then how they scalded the tongue and pierced the self. The scalding was a good reason for tears in the eyes.

'And where is she? Why didn't you bring her?'

'She's not with me; she's with her mother and father. I'll go there for our wedding which I want you all to come to. Don't forget, two months' time. Then I'll bring her home.'

'To live?'

'At Nanny's.'

'Nanny's! You've never been wrong!'

'It's what the old lady wants.'

'Not once, not ever!'

'And there's more news too,' my father said. 'Hemi's on his way back.'

'To stay?'

'With Ra and Mereana. None of their own kids will come so Ra asked him when he was home at Easter and he agreed.'

'With his wife and family.'

'Two girls and a boy, and they're all looking forward to it. They stayed a week at Easter and decided to come back for good even though Hemi's never done that sort of work before and Pam's a city girl. But Ra will teach them everything about the farm and he'll teach Hemi all he needs to know about the other things.'

'There'll be kids in the place again.'

'And once Toki starts ....'

'If he hasn't already ....'

'He hasn't but he can hardly wait. That's why I came here for some advice from my mate.'

'Who's too busy filling himself with mussels ....'

'Them that talks doesn't eat. Them that doesn't eat gets hungry.' He hadn't looked so happy for a long time.

Luckily my father and Toki had brought the mattress with them, but no matter how we shifted things about we couldn't find a space big enough for it. So at last we had to push it under our bed with only the top end showing, where their heads would be. Toki was just able to squeeze himself on to the small settee where my mother had been sleeping.

I persuaded them to stay a few days extra, and at the end of the time I told my mother to return with them. It wouldn't be easy to be without her but I knew my father needed her and I couldn't think of him going back to the house alone. 'I'm all right now,' I said. 'He's the one that needs you. I feel well, and the days until the baby arrives will soon pass.' She didn't know what to do but was at last persuaded that she should go. 'I'll bring her back next month,' my father said. 'In time for our baby. I'll get two weeks off work and we'll come and spend the two weeks with our grandchild.'

'We might have a bigger place by then.'

'You'll let us know the minute our grandchild arrives?'

'And ring,' she said. 'Ring if there's anything. But

there's no need to worry. It's a quiet place; I'm sure of that.'

'Mum and I will bring some more mussels and kina for you.'

'Yes, yes, never mind if your cousin gets the boot. They'll make sure to bring you some kai. Guess who has to jump in the sea! Guess who gets the sack!'

'You can't get the sack ....'

'... if you got no job.'

'And as soon as our grandchild arrives ....'

'We'll ring, we'll let you know as soon as we can, so you can both come.'

So you can both come, we'll let you know as soon as we can. The car was turning, squeezing into the line of traffic that was always passing, and those were the last words I said to him. So you can come. Waving from the kerb, our backs to the dark hole of the stairway. We'll let you know as soon as we can. Calling thinly into the din of engines, the pneumatic drill and the heels knocking, the slow fall of metal from a creeping truck.

It wasn't easy to see them go and I felt Graeme's anxiety as he turned from me to climb the stairs. But I was happy inside myself. Glad that I had been able to let her go, and glad to feel close to Graeme again. I was anxious to put the past months behind me so that together we could look forward to the baby. I was willing the time to pass.

I occupied myself easily enough with the few chores. And there were name-tabs to stitch on to small jackets and gowns, and a bag to pack and unpack. Count and sort and repack.

And there were books to read. Past the bakery and Take Away, the Tip Top, the fruit shop, secondhand shop, shoe shop, tobacconist, and bargain mart was the book exchange. Shelves of books, their covers battered and their pages thickened by constant fingering until they resembled sheets of discoloured wadding. I spent many hours there, looking along the shelves, delving into the ticketed bins — and many hours sitting by the window reading the stories and secrets that the books contained.

Also there was our quivering and tumbling baby to talk to, as the machines cracked into the roadway beneath me, and the tops of people's heads and the tips of their toes passed by.

One afternoon I climbed the cavern of stairs with my few parcels and books, and as I went in and shut the door behind me I was surprised at the sound of my own voice, singing.

21

'They haven't come yet?'

'Not yet, but they could be on the way. When I rang yesterday to say I'd brought you here she said they'd come as soon as they could. She said to ring when there was news.'

'Could be almost here if they left this morning' — this morning an age ago.

'Or they could wait until it's time for baby and me to come out, and spend their two weeks then.'

'If they're not there when I get back I'll ring again. Tried this morning after our baby was born but couldn't get through.'

'Then they must have left. And anyway it doesn't matter; it's just that they wanted to know. All I need is a good long sleep.'

'Like our baby is having right now.'

'Unlike before.'

'Screaming.'

'I think I yelled myself.' This morning.

'Why shouldn't you.'

'The smell, and everyone telling me what to do. That mask. Over my face .... If you hadn't been there ....'

'But I was' — an age ago.

'Breathe fast.'

'And faster.'

'Deeply.'

'Don't ....' Voices behind white cloth, and the room, the white room, stifling. Darkening and lightening. Revolving. 'Just one.' The noises were my own. 'Once more.' Then relief and a momentary quiet. 'A boy,' a masked voice said.

And when the voice said, 'A boy, you have a boy', it was about then that my father died — and I was so happy at that moment.

I was content seeing the boy, damp and crying, eyelids puffed and tightly closed, mouth opening and closing as the chest rose and fell, dispelling the blue-greyness from his skin. Content feeling the warmth and closeness at last, and listening to the newness of the crying. I heard myself give him my father's name but I didn't know my father was dead by then.

'I love you very much,' I said to Graeme.

'Then nothing else matters to me, nothing ever.' A bell tinkled in the corridor. 'I'll ring them when I get home but they could be almost here. Goodnight, my dearest, and my son.'

He called after school the next day, bringing oranges and books and something in a brown paper parcel, and said he knew of a house that he thought I would like. We would be able to move into it in a month's time if it was suitable. We talked and talked, planning our lives as we hadn't done for a long time. It was almost time for him to go before I asked, 'Did you ring, last night?'

'But I couldn't get a reply. I'll go now, and at tea-time I'll ring. There's sure to be someone there at tea-time, unless they're on their way. Then I'll come again afterwards and tell you. But maybe they're there now waiting.'

'Sitting on the stairs.'

'They can't come. Just yet.' And he looked away and was quiet. 'She said to give the baby your father's name.'

'I've done that already.' But he didn't look at me, so I thought about what he'd just said. 'He's ill,' I said, already knowing. And he wouldn't look at me, he wouldn't answer. So I said, 'He's dead' — because I already knew.

'I would have told you in the morning.'

'We'll have to be there by morning' — as the night descended.

22

'I can't,' I said. 'Not yet. There are things, several things, I have to do.'

'You don't want to go back?' Graeme said.

'I do, I will, but not yet. But you go and I'll come in another month.'

'Go with him now,' my mother said. 'Your Auntie Mereana will stay with me for a while. Lena too. Your Dad's gone and there's nothing more we can do ....'

'There's something else ....'

'I need you to come with me now. If you don't come now I know you never will.'

'In another month. I'll come in another month. It'll be easier if I have a little more time.'

'I could wait. A little longer?'

'It'll be harder for me to do what I've decided if you stay. I have to do right — now that it's the right time. But you will find it very hard — because of what's different between us, I wouldn't be able .... But after that ....'

'You'll come?'

'I'll come, more easy in my mind.'

I'd said my goodbyes silently during the hours and days we'd spent at his side, the exhausting grief-filled hours and days. The days which brought groups of visitors coming to speak to my father and to speak to us. To weep with us, press their noses on ours, and mingle their tears with our tears.

Yet the nights were quiet and comfortable, sleeping beside my father who lay in an adornment of fine cloaks and prized family possessions; at his head the photographs of those who had gone before.

There was warmth as the whole house breathed.

Also there were the needs of the boy to look to. The boy, who had his name, slept, woke to be fed and tended, then slept again, being passed from one to the other and held closely. But he and the boy had never known each other and this was the most difficult of all to bear.

'You breathed out as he breathed in so that now your breathing is his breathing. He stands where you have stood, and so he must walk where you have walked, and must know the things you would have wanted him to know. I wouldn't take him from you, or from her.

'The warmth that has gone from your body is close by, suffusing all. We will remember the warmth, but now we are exhausted. Our grief has exhausted us at last, the hours and days and nights of grief. So now, before the lid goes down, before the fall of earth which will be the final anguish, I can say what the others have been saying — "Go. Go then into the night, your night that is long and ever long. That is dark beyond measure and intensely dark. Go into this your ever longest and darkest of nights. It's all right. Go." '

Then earth clouting wood beneath the plying shovels. And above, the last wail and last moan fading.

'If it's what you want,' she said.

'It's what I want and it's what must be.'

'Then I'm happy, and so is your father, knowing his place won't be left empty.'

'His grandson's place is here with you.'

'Until it's my time to follow.'

'And another foothold for me on a place and a time. I'll come often.'

'But would you? Would you have done this if your father had still been here.'

'I'm not sure, but of course if you had asked.'

'We couldn't have asked.'

'Because of Graeme and of what's different between us.'

'It'll be hard for him.'

'The most difficult thing of all.'

'But you're very close to each other.'

'We're close to each other because he's had the strength, and now there's this. Will he be strong enough for this?'

'But you've had to be strong too, to be who you are.'

'I'm not sure.'

'Not sure?'

'That there's been a choice. Or if there was a choice then I made it long ago, perhaps at about the time we came home with the stone. Perhaps all our decisions are made at that young age, and maybe later ideas about what I wanted my life to be were only ideas after all. ... You remember that day, don't you? You were all frightened — you and Dad, Nanny, and Grandpa Toki, and the others. Scared of what the boy brought in and showed you.'

'You can't steal from the dead without harming the living. It wasn't ours, or his, to have.'

'But there was nothing you could have said to the man that would have helped him to know what you knew. And nothing he could have told you that would have persuaded you he was right.'

'One of us would have suffered, if not all.'

'And I knew. That's what I'm trying to say ....'

'That it should be returned and that we could suffer because of it.'

'Yes, I knew that too, most surely, and I still do. But I'm speaking of something else as well. I knew about differences ... that could never be resolved. It was all there in Nanny's kitchen that afternoon. People standing not an arm's length from each other, yet being so far apart.'

'And now you're thinking of your husband.'

'But I know something more now. I know it's possible to be close, and to love, and that even with differences you can be open to knowing. It's something I've learnt from Graeme. But now this: it will be the most difficult of all for him.'

'And it's time now for you to go to him.'

Later, although it was summer, I went to plant a tree, a ti kouka, beside the other one, and shaded from the sun's ferocity by the old one that stood behind, guarded by the one that stood before. I kept the soil firm and wet about the roots as I knew she would continue to do after I'd gone. She would care also for the boy I'd gently weaned and given to her. She would help nourish and strengthen him and lead him in his first steps over the ground where those who had gone before had given him the right to walk. And in having a place to stand he would have a place to step from and to return to when that future time came. As I had.

He would know an old woman who was the hill and the creek running through, and the treasure forever buried, and would be given the gifts that she had to give, which he would then hold for the ones to come.

He would know too a young man who has never once erred. Whose soul is dark glowing black. Stainless and shining, and as pure as the night of Mutuwhenua when the moon goes underground and sleeps.

So it was time for me to leave them. I could go without sadness, knowing my decision was the right one, and knowing there was one waiting for me, one of whom my mother had asked: 'Will he be strong enough for this?' But I went to him confidently. He had not once failed to love. I went, remembering that day of Rakaunui, the time when you can see the shape of the tree that Rona clutched as the moon drew her to the skies.

Glossary

haunga	stinking
jack nohi	nosy
kai moana	sea food
kakaho	type of pampas grass
kamokamo	marrow-like vegetable
kanga piro	fermented corn
kehua	ghost
kina	sea urchin
kuia	old woman
mimi	urinate
moko	tattoo
Mutuwhenua	phase of moon at which it is invisible
ngaio	small native tree with edible fruit
pahau	beard
piupiu	flax skirt
porangi	demented
puha	sow-thistle
Rakaunui	full moon
ti kouka	cabbage tree
toetoe	sedge (cutty) grass
tutae	excrement
waiata	song (n.), to sing (v.)

Rona

One night at full moon a woman called Rona was going to the spring to fill her calabashes when the moon was suddenly obscured by a passing cloud. Rona tripped and hurt herself, so she cursed the moon for having withdrawn its light. The moon heard her, came down and snatched her up, and began to carry her away. Rona caught at the branch of a ngaio tree and clung to it, but the tree got torn out by its roots and, with Rona, taken up to the sky and placed on the moon's surface. At full moon Rona can be seen, clutching the tree and her calabashes.